LOVING LANA

A Morgan Brothers Romance

LOVING LANA

•

Nancy J. Parra

AVALON BOOKS
NEW YORK

PRINTED IN THE UNITED STATES OF AMERICA
ON ACID-FREE PAPER
BY HADDON CRAFTSMEN, BLOOMSBURG, PENNSYLVANIA

For my parents, Ted and Frances Kozicki.
Thank you for your love and support and for always believing
in me.
I'm proud to call you Mom and Dad.

Chapter One

It was cold in the saloon where Lana Tate played a sprightly tune. She had wrapped her shawl around her shoulders and wore crocheted fingerless gloves to keep her hands as warm as possible. She knew the song well. It was one of her mother's favorites, and her mother had sung with the New York Metropolitan Opera. Some said that Lana had her mother's voice, the voice of an angel.

It was the only thing she had, so she used it to survive. Belting out the tune in a clear soprano, she knew she stopped everyone in the smoke-filled Wyoming saloon.

It had always been that way for Lana. Her small frame and delicate hands could coax music from any instrument, but her pixie face never caught a man's attention. Her hair was thin and almost silvery-blond. Her skin was the hue of pure cream. She had always

1

dreamed of having color, but even in her best worsted-wool dress she tended to blend into the woodwork.

Except when she sang. Then the very air seemed to stop and listen. Lana smiled and continued the happy song. When she sang in the saloon, she liked to pretend she was practicing for the opera and that, one day, someone famous would drop by and discover her.

The song ended and the men and women in the saloon applauded. Lana turned to the small crowd of regulars and bowed her head.

"You have the prettiest voice of anyone I have ever heard," Chance Landry said. "I swear Lana, with the right backing in the right city, you could be a star."

Lana smiled. Chance had been saying that since she started working at the saloon nearly three years ago, but he was full of talk. He could shoot the bull with the best, and Lana found out fast that if she ever wanted to get anywhere in her life, there was only one person that she could rely on—herself.

"A good tip will help me get there," she replied.

"Sweetlin', that was my tip," Chance said with a wink. They both knew that if he had a good night, he'd leave a little something in her tip jar. So she played well and prayed that Chance would win big.

"I got news!" an old cowboy crowed as he pushed into the saloon. "The reward on catchin' that there wild stallion has been capped at two grand, boys, an' it's all gonna be mine."

Someone let out a wolf whistle. "Hey, Sam, two grand will build you a mansion in downtown Denver. You gonna invite us to come visit?"

The cowboy grinned proudly and stepped up to the bar. "Git yer own mansion," he hollered back. "As fer me, I'm headin' out first thing in the mornin'. Tell ya what, when I git back I'll buy ya a round of drinks. Right now I'm just buyin' fer myself." He waved to the bartender and put down a coin.

Lana glanced toward the bar. Two thousand dollars was a lot of money. Enough that she could take her pa and move out of Wyoming. Enough to pursue her dreams of singing in a real opera just like her mother had.

"What's so special about this horse?" she asked the men gathered around. There had to be a catch to a bet that big or someone would have cashed in on it already.

"Why, little lady, that stallion's so smart an' so ornery that no one in three states has ever been close to catchin' him," Sam said, downed his shot of rot gut and wiped his mouth on his sleeve. "Until me, that is. I got me a secret plan."

"Secret plan or no secret plan, you won't get him," Chance said as he stepped away from the gaming tables. "There's only one man who's got a chance at that horse an' that's Taggart Morgan."

"Who's Taggart Morgan?" Lana asked, her curiosity piqued.

"Why, he's the best danged horseman this side of the Mississippi," Hal told her. "He's been tracking that old stallion for two years now. That's why the reward's grown so big. It's startin' to look like even Tag Morgan can't catch him."

"Hmmm. So all the winner has to do is catch the horse? They don't have to break him?"

Chance smiled his smooth gambler's smile. "All they have to do is catch him, sweetlin'. But the reward is just the beginning. That horse would fetch another five grand at auction even unbroke."

"That must be some animal," Lana said.

"It is," Chance replied. "To catch him a body's going to have to be clever, quick, and pure horse genius. My money's on Morgan."

"I'll take that bet," Sam said with a toothless grin. "I'll lay down a fiver that I'll bring him in myself within the month. My secret plan is that good."

"I don't think so," Chance said and put a bill down on the bar. "Hal, hold this for us. Sam, we'll meet back here in one month and see who's collecting the money."

Lana sighed with momentary disappointment and turned back to the piano. That five could have been her tip for the night if Sam hadn't come into the saloon. Now she was going to go home with only a few pennies and whatever Hal gave her to stay after and wash up.

But the talk of this stallion got her to thinking. If she won that reward and then sold the horse, she would be free from this small town. Free to go all the way to San Francisco if she wanted to, a place where she'd never have to worry about cold fingers, crops that didn't grow, and hungry livestock that needed feeding.

She stared at her sheet music, her thoughts on catching a wily horse. She had to admit she didn't know enough to do it. Not yet, anyway.

Her fingers danced along the keys as she played a familiar tune. She smiled as the answer to her problem came to her. Maybe she was stuck here now, she thought. But she wouldn't be stuck for long. If Chance had it right, there was one man who had the answers she needed. All she had to do was convince Taggart Morgan to teach her how to catch a horse.

Taggart was up before the dawn. It was a cold, clear fall morning. The sky threatened to snow. He took a deep breath and exhaled with enthusiasm as he walked to the stable. Fall was his favorite time of year. He could see his breath now, but he knew by the afternoon it would be warm enough that he'd have to shed the layers of clothing he wore.

The ground crunched under his feet. The frost had been early this year, turning the leaves into bright colors overnight.

The mountains were dark against the early morning sky. Pale rays of sun peeked over the horizon, painting the mountaintops a pale pink in a sea of deep blue.

"Morning, Tag," Henry Beaumont said when Tag entered the stable. Tag smiled at his friend. Henry was considered the second finest horseman in the state. Tag's father had rescued him from a bad situation, and in return Henry had sworn to remain loyal to the Morgan ranch, the Bar M.

"How'd Cheyenne do last night?" Tag asked as he

strode to the stall nearest the tiny tack room where Henry had insisted on spending the night.

"That old horse has more gump in him than sense," Henry said. "I think you'll be able to use him at least another year."

"I won't need him that long."

"What'cha figurin' on doing?" Henry asked.

"Right now, I'm going to head into town and pick up some supplies. Then I'm off to the backcountry. This is it, Henry, I'm going to bring that black stallion home," Tag said with confidence.

Henry smiled and patted Cheyenne's nose. "I wondered what was taking you so long."

"I was waiting to see how high the reward would go."

"It's up to two thousand, isn't it?"

"Yep, I heard tell they capped it at that," Tag said, "and I need a new stallion."

Henry shook his head. "Everybody knows you're the best horseman in Wyoming. Heck, maybe in the whole United States. You're darn near a sure bet."

"Yes, but I haven't brought him in yet and people have begun to believe he can't be caught."

"He's one wild horse, smarter than Satan an' just as ornery. I've seen him from a distance. You're going to have to be better than you ever were if you're going to capture and keep him."

"I'll get him," Tag said and grabbed his saddle off its shelf. "I got a plan." He opened the door to his favorite mare's stall. "Tell my brothers not to worry about me unless I'm not back in a month."

"Gotcha," Henry said. "How come you're not taking Thunder? Doesn't he have better footing in the mountains?"

Tag stopped saddling his horse and smugly turned to his good friend. "It's all part of the plan."

Henry scratched his head. "It is?" He nodded toward the mare. "Ain't Thunder faster than that mare?"

Tag smiled and finished saddling up. "Now Henry, I'm surprised at you. Especially after watching my brothers these past few months. Seems you might have learned something."

Henry frowned. "What?"

"My lovely sisters-in-law have taught me a good lesson. The right woman can make a man crazy. Maybe even crazy enough to follow her right into my corral." Tag led the mare out of her stall.

"Is that what you figure on doing to the black stallion?"

"Exactly," Tag said. "I plan on letting Sunshine here drive him just mad enough that I can get my hands on him. The way I figure it, this prime little mare is the perfect thing to bring our boy in. You watch: within a month, Sunshine will have that old boy eating out of my hand."

Tag strode out into the morning light and mounted. Heart filled with anticipation, he glanced over the horizon at the rising sun. He had nearly twenty good breeding horses. With the stallion he'd be able to start bloodlines that would match those of any Kentucky animal.

"I'll take good care of your animals," Henry said.

"Be sure to give Thunder enough exercise. That gelding isn't going to be too happy when I bring the old boy back."

"I'll take care of it. Good luck," Henry said and saluted Tag.

Tag whirled his mare around and cantered across the frosted prairie. If his observations were correct, then all it took to get an ornery male to toe the line was the right female. He was certain Sunshine was it. He'd have that wily stallion in less than a month. Tag smiled broadly. Or sooner.

"Lana, what are you doing, girl? Where's my breakfast?"

Lana no longer cringed at the slight slur in her father's voice. He hadn't been sober a day since her mother died six years ago. That was why she had taken the job playing in the saloon. It allowed her to buy enough supplies to get them through the winters.

"Daddy, there's eggs on the stove and fresh biscuits cooling on the table," she called to him. She carefully dressed in a sturdy split skirt and her father's old leather jacket. Then she wrapped a pair of extra underthings in a pillowcase along with her hairbrush, toothbrush, and her mother's locket.

"I can't find a clean bowl," he hollered back. "What are you doing?"

Lana climbed down from her loft and eyed her father. Dressed in his union jack and a pair of slacks, he looked old, tired, and helpless. It was hard to hide the pity she felt. What her ma had seen in Jeff Tate,

Lana would never know, but whatever it was had made her mother give up the glamour and comfort of her life as a premier singer at the Met. It had made her marry a struggling rancher.

Pa had been unlucky in most everything but love. They had traveled from state to state, buying into one scam after another until her mother had taken ill. Then they bought this piece of useless land and here they remained.

The only thing her father did now was tend her mother's grave and drink. Lana had been angry at first, but after awhile had come to accept her lot in life.

Somehow she had known this wouldn't always be the way of it. And now she had a way out. If she caught that horse she would have enough money to move to a sophisticated city like San Francisco and maybe, just maybe, be the voice that was the toast of the town.

"Lana, there's not a single clean bowl," her father whined. "I swear I thought you said you did the dishes."

"I did," she said. "Here." She pulled a bowl down from the cupboard and filled it with the egg potato mix. "Sit. Let me get this for you."

Her father sat with a huge sigh and smiled at her. His watery eyes were bloodshot from so many years of drink. Lana half-believed he was trying to kill himself to join her mother. She put the bowl down in front of him, handed him a spoon, and sat down.

He dove into the meal as if he hadn't eaten in two days. Lana watched him as he wolfed it down, never stopping long enough to chew. Egg dripped down his scraggly bearded chin as he grabbed a biscuit and shoved it in his mouth. She sighed.

"Pa, I have something to tell you."

"What is it?" he mumbled, his mouth full, his attention solely on his bowl.

"Pa, I'm going to be going away for awhile," she said with determination.

He looked up then, chewing with his mouth full. "What?!"

"I said I was going away for awhile."

Her father got a vague but frightened look in his eyes. "Why?"

"There's something I want to do."

"Can't you do it here?"

"No."

"Who will cook? Who will clean?"

She took a deep breath. "I've asked Mrs. March to stop by for a few hours each day."

"Who's that?"

"She's a very nice widow I met in town."

"What's a widow want with housekeeping?"

"She has five children to support."

"You paying her?"

"Of course."

"Stupid. Stay home, we could use the money."

"Pa, I'm leaving for a few weeks. You will simply have to take care of yourself until I get back."

Lana stood up. Her father looked bewildered. He was not an angry drunk. He was merely helpless, but if she stayed here, she would die an old maid. That was not what she wanted for her life.

Her pa had taken care of the family before her mother died. It was time he started taking care of himself again. She kissed him on the cheek. "I'll be back soon."

"I'll be dead."

"You'll be fine." She picked up her bundle and headed toward the door. "Remember, Mrs. March will be checking in on you."

"You shouldn't waste your money."

"She's a widow, Pa. She needs the money."

"You walk out that door and you've as good as killed me."

" 'Bye, Pa, I'll see you in a few weeks." Lana closed the door softly behind her. She swallowed the guilt that her father had made her feel, but she knew she must leave. She was eighteen years old, and this could be her only chance at having a life.

Besides, she thought as she raced to the barn, once she caught that horse then her father could live in luxury, and neither one of them would ever have to worry again.

Tag double-checked that the burlap sacks of provisions were evenly distributed. He had gotten into town in record time. The stores were newly opened and he was able to purchase what he needed without too many prying eyes. Tag knew that everyone in the area would be out after that stallion. He hoped to buy himself a little lead time.

"Excuse me, are you Taggart Morgan?"

Tag glanced over his shoulder. A little bitty gal

stood there looking at him with the biggest green eyes he'd ever seen.

"Last time I checked I was," he answered, then continued to check his saddle.

"Good, I've been looking for you."

He sighed and leaned against his saddle. "I swear I didn't do it, honey. You're probably looking for one of my brothers."

A small frown formed on her pixie face. "I'm looking for the Morgan they say is the best horseman in three states. Is that you?"

Tag turned back to his saddle and packs. "Now that is a matter of opinion." He moved to the other side and adjusted the packs. "So say I'm the best horseman in the country." He paused and looked at her. "Why are you looking for a horseman?"

"I need to learn about wild horses," she said.

Taggart thought that was the oddest thing he'd ever heard from a little gal on a chilly morning. "Ike over at the stables can point you toward a good teacher."

She walked around his horse. "I don't want just any teacher," she said. "I need the best teacher."

"Why?"

"I want to catch that wild stallion."

Taggart couldn't help it. He just had to laugh. The idea of this little bit of a thing catching that wily old beast was just more than he could take. It struck his funny bone.

"I don't see what's so funny," she said. Her big eyes narrowed and she planted her hands on her hips. The wind whipped around her and Tag, chafing her cheeks and nose to a pale pink. Her anger and the wind brought color to her, making her look like a fairy queen buzzing in anger at one of her subjects.

Tag tried to swallow his laughter. "Honey, that horse is ten times your size. I swear, he'd be the one to catch you, not the other way around."

"Do you want to teach me or not?" she asked, determination in her voice. "I'll pay you."

He eyed her old oversized coat and worn split skirt. Her half boots were cleaned and shined, but he could almost make out the shape of her feet through the thin toes. "What do you plan on paying me with? Hmmm? Fairy dust?" He snorted at his own joke.

She gave him a dark look, her silver eyebrows lowering, her fisted hands shaking. "I am willing to give you fifty dollars."

He stopped chuckling and gave her a serious look. "Fifty dollars is a lot of money."

"It's a small amount compared to two grand. I believe it is worth the investment."

She looked so small and so helpless, his heart kind of melted. He chucked her under the chin. "Honey, the best investment would be for you to take that money and buy a new set of clothes and supplies to get you through the winter."

"Don't touch me like that," she said and jerked her head away. "I'm a grown woman and I know what's best for me. Right now, I'm asking for you to teach me horse skills."

Tag untied his mare from the hitching post. "Sorry, I don't have the time." He stepped up into his saddle and her anger fled from her face, momentarily replaced with desperation.

"Then how about giving me a few tips? I swear it won't take more than half a day."

"Nope," Tag said simply and pulled the reins so his horse headed down the street.

The little gal kept right in step with him. "I'll give you ten dollars for ten tips."

"Nope."

"Five for five?"

"Nope."

She was near to running. "Just one tip, Mr. Morgan."

"Go home."

"That's not a tip," she said and stopped in her tracks.

Tag kept going a few feet, but his conscience got the better of him. He blew out a breath and looked back. She stood in the street looking like she'd lost her best friend. "Well, heck." He turned Sunshine back and came up next to the gal. "I'll give you two tips for free."

She looked up at him with eager hope in her expressive eyes.

"First off, don't wave that fifty dollars around town or you'll find yourself in a bad situation. Second, horses are a bit like people. They like sweet things and soft words."

That said, Tag took off at a canter. He refused to look back. He'd done his best to advise her. Right now he had a stallion to catch.

Chapter Two

"**A**rrogant man."

Lana stuffed her money back in her belt. She watched the big man canter out of town as if he had the whole world in his sights. From the look of him he probably did. She sighed. It didn't do any good to hold onto her anger. It was quite clear that he didn't take her seriously. "Fine, don't help me," she muttered. "I'll just do it by myself."

How, she still wasn't sure. Ike at the stable wouldn't do her any good. She'd had her own horse, Penny, for the past four years. She knew how to ride and care for the animal. What she didn't know was how to track and catch a wild one. Well, she wouldn't let that stop her. If Sam Gooding thought he could catch the stallion, then she knew she could do it.

She glanced at the general store. Wouldn't Taggart Morgan be surprised when she beat him at his own

15

Mexico - Audrain County Library
305 West Jackson
Mexico, Missouri 65265

game? Especially when she could tell him she used his advice. Smiling and humming to herself, Lana went into the building. She came out twenty minutes later with a pocket full of sugar cubes, supplies, and a head full of stories about where the horse had been spotted.

She packed and mounted Penny and headed out of town in the same direction Taggart had gone. He might be considered the best horseman out there, but she had something he didn't have: determination.

Her whole future depended on capturing that horse and she would do whatever it took to make that happen, using sweet talk and sugar cubes.

After a week on the trail, Tag found himself in an obscure little canyon on the edge of the stallion's territory.

So far, Sunshine had been little help. He blew out a long breath. Surely the old boy would have noticed them by now. What was keeping him?

The afternoon air was brisk in the higher elevations as Tag followed the stallion's harem of mares.

He tracked the group over a ridge and down into a wooded valley. Pausing, he frowned at the tracks. Amidst the prints was one pair of shod feet. That meant either someone had lost a horse to the stallion or someone else had invaded Tag's territory.

Consternation filled him. He couldn't have that. There was a sizable reward for the safe capture of the animal, and he wasn't about to lose. Besides, they didn't call him the best horseman in the state for nothing. He knew the animal so well he could almost hear him think.

Tag checked the tracks again. The horse with shoes ran with the herd. That meant it was more likely the horse was a runaway. Still, he unlatched the cover on his six-shooter just in case.

Tag walked his mare along the edge of the ridge. As far as he could see, the group had gone into the valley and had not come back out. That was a very good sign.

He eased through the aspen trees. The ground was drier here and his mare kicked up the scent of moss and decaying leaves. The yellowing aspens quaked like a shiver of water and he took a deep breath.

Tag knew he enjoyed the sensual aspects of the land. He may have taken pride in being the most un-civilized of the Morgan brothers, but secretly he was drawn to the textures of the world. He reveled in the sight of the sunlight against the golden leaves and bright blue sky.

He inhaled the scent of earth and sky and knew he was more comfortable here than he was at the ranch. Now that his brothers were married, he found he really didn't have a place any more.

Tag had hoped capturing the stallion would give him enough of a nest egg to purchase land to the north and start a ranch of his own. He'd made a pretty de-cent living on the sale of his horses so far, but he wanted more . . . he wanted a place of his own.

Tag was roused out of his musings by a faint sound. He stopped his horse and stood up in his stirrups. He turned his keen ears toward the sound. It was haunting and beautiful, like the sound of an angel that had fallen to earth.

Tag crept closer. Bright, clear notes danced along the air, causing gooseflesh to rise up on his arms. If he didn't know better, he'd swear he was hearing one of the sirens from that book he had read, Homer's *Iliad*.

He broke through the brush and caught sight of the source of the beautiful notes. A young woman sat on a boulder. Sunlight bounced off her fine white-blond hair. Her pixie face and soulful voice touched Tag's heart in a way no other ever had.

It was as if he had been hit by lightning. He wondered if he blinked, would she disappear? She was strangely dressed for an angel. She wore an oversized fringed coat, suede split skirt, and heavy boots.

But those beautiful notes were coming out of her mouth. Sheer awe drew him across the field as if he were in a dream. His heart carried him forward.

He realized he'd seen this gal before. She was the same one that offered to pay him if he taught her how to catch the stallion. Dagummit, why hadn't he noticed how pretty she was? Maybe it was her ridiculous request that threw him off. Or maybe it was the poor condition of her clothing.

He shrugged. It didn't matter, really. Pretty or not, it was clear to him that she was stubborn. She probably followed him out here to try to get him to teach her about horses.

He needed to have a talk with this little lady. Stubborn or not, it wasn't right for a gal like her to be wandering alone in the backcountry. She should be home, baking biscuits or practicing the piano. Whatever it was that young gals did all day. Tag figured he was the only one around to point this out. So it looked like he was stuck with the job.

Heck. He realized that he didn't even know her name.

Tag eased Sunshine into the field and noticed more than the gal on the rock. He noticed what, or rather who, also seemed curious about her singing. The wild black stallion of legend stood not more than one hundred feet from her.

He watched as the stallion eased forward, nostrils flared, eyes curious. Tag held his breath. The horse was passive for the moment, but that gal had no idea what she was doing. A wild animal like the stallion was fierce. If he was to get spooked or caught scent of anything wrong, he would flail out with his sharp hooves. In essence, he could kill her with a few blows.

The stallion edged toward her warily, but she just kept singing as if she were a lady on the stage of a grand opera house. Pure terror burst through him when she reached out to stroke the stallion's muzzle.

The little gal was either fearless or just plain ignorant of wild things. He figured it was ignorance. The stallion's posture was wary as he blew out a snort. The action must have startled her because she gasped and quit singing.

The hairs on the back of Tag's neck stood on end. He was about to witness a tragedy. He must have groaned. The sound coming out of him caused the horse and woman to turn. They reacted instantly. She jumped up—which was the wrong thing to do around a wild horse. Startled, the stallion flared his nostrils and pawed the ground. He was about to attack.

Instinct kicked in, and Tag took off after the stallion. The animal reared, his flailing hooves barely missing the gal. Tag hollered to distract him.

The old boy let out a territorial scream, turned on his haunches and raced across the valley floor. He was fast. Faster than Sunshine could ever be.

Tag pushed Sunshine to race after the stallion anyway. If he could get within ten feet of the old boy, he could have him.

They raced across the short valley floor. Tag grabbed his rope off the side of his saddle and twirled a lasso. He managed to get Sunshine within twenty feet of the stallion, but it wasn't meant to be. The animal snorted and kicked up his heels just before he sprinted up the mountain.

Tag knew it wouldn't be safe for Sunshine to follow. She didn't have good footing at high speeds. The last thing he needed right now was to hurt his mare.

So he slowed down.

Blowing out a long slow breath, Tag knew he had lost this time. But the chase had only begun. He turned back toward the edge of the valley where the woman had been. He needed to have a talk with the gal and he needed to have it now. His determined gaze roamed over the valley floor.

She was gone.

Tag took a deep breath and frowned. He knew better than to think she had realized the danger and was now headed home. If there was one thing his sister-in-laws had taught him, it was that once a woman got an idea in her head, it would take more than one narrow escape to change her mind.

Lana scrambled for cover. It was the only thing she could think of doing. Taggart Morgan had come out of nowhere and chased off the black stallion. She had a feeling that when he didn't catch the stallion he'd come looking for her. The last thing she wanted was for him to find her.

She rushed to her horse and took off. In the last few years, Lana had become rather good at hiding. Ever since she took the job in the saloon, she had learned to be careful. Sometimes men would try to follow her home. She knew it wasn't necessarily their fault. Men got funny ideas about a girl who sang in a saloon. She had learned to deal with it.

Glancing over her shoulder, she saw that Tag was still chasing the stallion. She reached the top of the ridge and dismounted. Then she patted her mare on the flank. Her horse knew the signal. Penny headed toward the small group of mares that the stallion had rounded up, and Lana took off in the opposite direction, leaping from boulder to boulder so as not to leave any footprints. Then she ducked down between two large rocks and squeezed into a tight crevice.

Thank goodness it was cold now. She knew that snakes often hid in crevices like this, but the chill in the air made them slow. She would just have to be quicker than any animal she might encounter. Luckily the crevice was empty and she settled into the twilight of the rocky shadows. Her heart raced with uncertainty for her safety and she hugged her knees. Taggart Morgan was a big man, and at the moment he didn't seem too happy. She blew out a breath.

Come to think of it, she wasn't very happy either. She had been so close to coaxing the stallion into eating out of her hand. Once she had him doing that it would only be a short time before she could slip a bridle over his head. Then it would be an easy trip back to town.

The presence of this man ruined everything.

She frowned. Maybe it had been a chance encounter. Maybe in a few days he would give up trying for the stallion. Yeah, and maybe she was the Queen of England. Lana knew from experience that nothing was ever that simple.

Then she heard it: the sound of boots walking on boulders. She held her breath as the sound got closer. Surely he couldn't track her on granite.

Could he?

The hairs on the back of her neck rose as the steps stopped above her. She pulled her skinning knife out of her boot and squeezed as far back in the crevice as she could.

"Hello?" a strong male voice called above her. "Look, I know you're in there. Come out."

She held as still as a rabbit. He was probably bluffing. There was no way he knew for sure where she was.

"It's stupid for you to hide. I know where you are."

She closed her eyes, her mind running over escape possibilities.

"Okay, I can see you're scared. You don't know me that well, but I swear I won't hurt you. My ma raised me with enough sense to look out for little gals like you."

She ground her teeth. She might be small but she was far from little. It was always the same with men. They never really saw her.

Silence danced between them. She swore she could hear him breathing. She clutched her knife.

"Look, I'm not going anywhere, so you might as well come out. I can and will wait you out."

She wanted to kick something. The man was no gentleman. A gentleman would offer assistance and then leave when it was refused.

"Okay, your choice," he said. "I'll just make myself comfortable."

Lana listened to his every move. It sounded like he was making camp, but she knew better. The rocks were huge here. There wasn't much room to sit, let alone make camp. The man was bluffing. Either that, or he was crazy.

Great. All she needed was to be hounded by a crazy man. She should have known better than to listen to Sam and Chance. She should have never hunted Taggart Morgan down.

Curious, she listened. It was quite odd how she

knew his every move. She could almost picture him as he brushed and hobbled his horse.

"Hey," he said, startling her. "I'm going to collect some firewood. If you think you're fast enough you can try to make a run for it, but I doubt you'd get very far."

Arrogant man. She wasn't falling for that. For all she knew he would silently wait for her to bolt. No, she would wait him out. Besides, darkness would allow her to slip away just fine. She had a lot going for her. She was small and light and wouldn't make a sound.

The only way he would know she left was if he slept over her crevice. The man might be crazy, but no one was that insane.

Tag shook his head. She was still playing rabbit. He knew she was tucked back into the boulders. The Morgan brothers were great trackers. It was said they could track a beetle on granite.

He knew precisely where she was but he was going to wait. She had to come out sometime, and he didn't have anything else to do at the moment. The stallion wouldn't let him get within a half mile now. The old boy knew he was being hunted and he would be more cautious.

Tag gathered firewood, keeping the entrance to her hidey-hole always within his peripheral vision. He didn't think she'd try to come out, but he was ready just in case.

It was an interesting situation. In fact, in all his born

days he'd never had a day like today. He felt like he had been thrown into one of his mother's fairy tales. The one where the beautiful princess lures the unicorn out of hiding.

Only he was lured as well. He didn't like it. He didn't like the way he had reacted to the sight of her. He knew he had to talk to her, to make her human, to dispel the magic that surrounded her.

He tried to keep in mind that she was just a stubborn little gal with a beautiful voice. She couldn't get him to help her with money, so she was trying to lure him with music. How she knew he liked that sort of thing, he didn't have a clue, but he was smarter than that and on his guard.

Tag took an armload of wood and built a small campfire on the flattest boulder. He leaned against one rock, dug through his saddlebag, and pulled out fixings for dinner.

The sunlight faded and he knew it was going to get cold. She had to be getting restless. The crevice she had stuffed herself into was small and cramped. Maybe he could lure her out with a hot meal.

He placed a cast-iron skillet on the flames and let it heat. He'd been working in silence, but he knew she was still there. He could hear her breathing.

"I have bacon," he said. "I'm going to make biscuits and gravy. You're more than welcome to join me."

He paused and listened to her breathing. It was almost as if he could read her mind. He swore at the silence and said, "Forget it!"

"Okay, your loss." He proceeded to cook dinner.

"The biscuits are good," he said. "It's my ma's recipe, but interestingly enough it was our pa that taught us how to cook on the trail. He said if you could make a fancy dinner out of trail fixings then you'd be set for life."

Tag stirred flour and water into the drippings for gravy. "But then again I never figured I'd spend dinner with a boulder."

He paused again to listen and cocked his head. He swore he heard her stomach growling as the scent of dinner wafted toward the crevice. He picked up the pan and brought it closer to the crack. Then just for good measure he waved the steam her way.

"I swear this is about the tastiest batch of biscuits and gravy I've made in a long time. Sure you don't want any?"

Silence greeted his question.

"Quit being so stubborn and come on out. I need to talk to you about how stupid it was of you to get so close to the stallion I'm chasing."

"You're not chasing him, I am."

Tag blinked. He wasn't sure if he really heard that or if he only thought it. "So, you think you're going to catch him. I thought you didn't know anything about horses. Isn't that why you came to Amesville to find me? Wasn't that you who said you'd pay me to teach you?"

His questions were met with silence. "Why don't you come out of there and tell me how you think you're now capable of catching the old beast?"

His request was met by more silence. He thought

for a moment he had just imagined her response. "Come on, dinner's getting cold."

"How do I know I can trust you?" came the musical reply from deep within the boulders.

"Well now, you don't, do you?" he answered simply and moved back to the fire before the gravy congealed any further. "You didn't know that when you came to town looking for a teacher either. So the way I figure it, you're just going to have to make a leap of faith."

"I have a weapon and I know how to use it."

"Of course you do." He snagged a second tin plate from his saddlebag and broke two biscuits open, then poured gravy on them. Then he pushed the plate toward the sound of her voice. "Better get that before it turns cold. I'd hate to ruin a good meal."

He fixed his own plate and pretended to ignore her. It was all a pretense though. He had the plate always in his sight, but he moved slowly and sat away from it. It was like coaxing a wild animal out of its den. He didn't make any sudden moves.

She crept out and crouched down. Firelight shone off the edge of a fair-sized blade. Tag figured it made her feel safe, so he let her keep it. That was, unless she tried to use it.

"Stay away from me," she said.

"Stand up and stretch," he commanded, keeping his attention on his plate so as not to spook her. "You have to be cramped, you've been in there for hours."

"I'm fine," she said and picked up the plate. He watched her eye the food suspiciously.

"Oh come on, I told you I wouldn't hurt you."

"Right." She pushed the plate away.

Impatient, he blew out a deep breath and reached over and traded her plate with his. She backed halfway into the crevice when he moved.

"Now eat," he ordered. "It's getting cold out and you'll need something warm in your stomach. Goodness knows you don't have much flesh to warm your bones."

She snagged his plate and sat down on a boulder that was just above and to the left of him. "I've been out here for days and haven't frozen yet."

"Really, days? How'd you get so close to the ornery old beast so quickly?"

She shrugged and scooped a spoonful of biscuit and gravy into her mouth.

He waited through the silence as she chewed.

"I've been easing my way into his harem," she said when her mouth was finally empty. "This was the first time I actually saw him."

"I heard you singing."

"I figured that."

"I guess the old saying that music soothes the savage beast is true."

"Maybe," she said and took another spoonful. "A handful of sugar cubes doesn't hurt either."

They ate in cautious silence. When Tag was finished, he wiped off his plate and put it with the pan to be cleaned later. Then he leaned back against his boulder and studied her. She was right pretty in the firelight. Like an angel. Her skin was smooth and pale. Her cheekbones where high in an oval face. Her hair was so fine and light it seemed to form a halo around her head. It picked up the faint starlight and shimmered against the blue-black of the clear night sky.

"What's your name?" he asked when she had taken her last bite.

"Lana," she answered. "Lana Tate."

Chapter Three

"Where do you live, Lana Tate?"

"No."

"No?"

"No, I don't have to tell you anything else. Just like you didn't have anything to teach me."

"I see," he said and grinned at the absurdity of her answer. "You want things all square between us."

"Yes," she said and wiped out her plate before she pushed it toward him. "I want everything to be square between us."

"Now that isn't very likely," he said as he took the plate. "To begin with, I'm about twice your size. Though I'd have to say your voice is twice the size of mine. Then there's the whole dinner issue. I cooked it. You ate it. Sweetheart, we'll never be even."

"Don't call me sweetheart," she demanded, displeasure coloring her tone.

"Why not?"

"No more answers." She stood up and stretched. He couldn't help but stare. His mouth popped open and every hair on his body stood at attention. She was not thin like he originally thought, but lithe and curvy in all the right places. Places that made Tag's palms itch.

"Don't do that," he growled.

"Do what?"

"Stretch like that."

"You were the one who told me to stretch."

"Well, I take it back. Don't do that."

She remained standing and leaned back against the bolder. "You are a very contrary man."

"What's wrong with that?"

"It's uncivilized."

Pride filled him and he grinned big. "You are one smart girl." Then he stood and picked up the dirty dishes. She remained where she was, but he swore she flinched. "Since I cooked, I think it's only fair that you do the dishes. To even things up, that is."

"They're your dishes. You wash them."

His grin widened. "Not much of a pushover are you."

"Only where contrary, uncivilized men are concerned," she said. "You give an inch and they take a mile. There will be no mile from me."

"I suppose you plan on slipping away when I turn my back to wash these dishes."

"Maybe."

"Then maybe I'll let them sit a bit longer." Taggart slid back down to his seat by the fire.

"You are a cruel man."

"That's me, cruel and contrary. Now, let's talk about you."

"What do you want to know about me?"

"Where do you come from?"

"My pa owns a place near Hunter."

"What's he do?"

"Drinks, mostly," she said softly.

Tag didn't like the sound of that. "Who takes care of you?"

"I do."

"I suppose you take care of your pa, too."

"Only since my ma died."

"How long ago was that?"

"About six years," she said and shrugged. "I'm over it."

Tag felt the need to do something with his hands. It near killed him to know this delicate creature had been fending for herself for six years. What she needed was someone to take care of her. No wonder she hid in crevices. "Look, I'm going to do a bit of whittlin', so don't run screaming when I pull out my knife."

She snorted. "I'm not afraid of your knife."

He raised an eyebrow at her bravado. "Good." He grabbed a thin branch from the pile of firewood and pulled his knife out of the sheath on his belt.

The only sound was the snapping of the fire and the smooth splicing of his knife into the soft wood.

"So, how old are you?"

"What difference does that make?"

It made a heck of a lot of difference. He didn't like these bizarre emotions that ran through him. He'd like it even worse if this gal was a child. He looked at her. "If you're under sixteen then you're a runaway and it's my responsibility to take you back home to your pa."

"I was twelve when my ma died."

He really looked at her then. "That makes you—"

"Eighteen," she said. "Old enough to take care of myself, my pa, and that stallion."

"That stallion darn near killed you today."

"He wouldn't have reared if you hadn't spooked him."

"That's not what I saw."

"Really? Just what did you see?"

"I saw you stupidly reach up to pat that animal's muzzle. That spooked him and he flailed out, darn near smacking you senseless."

"Well, I'm in no danger of that."

"What?"

"Sounds like you already think I'm senseless, so there was no danger of the stallion knocking me that way."

Tag grinned. He decided he liked her smart tongue almost as much as he liked her voice.

"A little gal like you should not be alone in the backcountry. It's not safe."

"I can take care of myself."

Tag snorted at that.

"Besides," she continued. "I've decided to listen to your advice."

"Good."

"I'm not wasting my money on teachers. I'm going to do this on my own using good old common sense, sweet talk, and a pocket full of sugar cubes."

Tag's jaw dropped. She really was crazy. "You're going to wind up dead."

"Then that's a chance I'm willing to take and, since I'm looking out for myself, there's no one to say otherwise."

"I say otherwise."

She shrugged. "You don't own me, this land, or that horse, so you have no say."

"Honey, I'm a man. That gives me say."

She raised an eyebrow at him. "Sounds to me like you're the one with a lot to learn."

Tag dug his knife into the branch. He had a nagging thought that maybe, just maybe, she was right. Time to approach this problem from another angle.

"So, what was that you were singing?"

She seemed startled by the question. "What?"

"What was the song you were singing?"

"It was from an opera," she said simply.

"An opera? Where'd you learn it?"

"My ma sang in the New York Metropolitan Opera."

"I see," he said, curious, and sliced deeper into the branch. "How'd you end up out here?"

She slid down then and sat. Her arms were crossed over her chest, bringing the big coat in tight around her. "I guess my pa's a bit of a dreamer. He married ma and headed out for the glory land." She sighed. "He just never found it."

Tag wanted to throttle something. This sweet creature belonged safe and happy in a fancy house in New York. Her pa was a fool.

"You got any other family?"

"Some in New York, but they disowned my ma when she married pa."

"I see."

She shrugged and huddled deeper into her coat. "We didn't need them or their money."

He let that settle into the crisp night air for a moment. Her tone spoke volumes, filled with emotions of hurt and betrayal. He had to concentrate on his carving to keep from grabbing her and holding her in his arms. If he did that she would surely run screaming from him. Right now this gal was as wild as that stallion.

"You look cold," he said, finally breaking the silence. "Why don't you come in closer to the fire? I swear I won't move."

"I've seen you move," she said. "You're too quick for my liking."

He blew out a breath. "Fine, I'm warm, I'm going to move away from the fire and try to get some sleep."

Tag got up, grabbed his blanket and moved off the boulder. He sat down on the dry ground, tossed his blanket over him, and rested his hat over his eyes.

He listened to her breathing. She seemed indecisive. He knew she was cold. Even if she ran he could catch her, and he figured she was smart enough to know it.

He hoped she would at least have sense enough to get closer to the fire.

It took all of two minutes before she moved. He heard her rub her hands together and imagined that she held them out to warm.

"So, what made you decide you needed to hunt the old beast?" Tag asked.

She shifted as if startled by his words, but then slowly relaxed when she saw that he did not move. "The two grand."

Tag frowned into the depths of his Stetson. "What do you want with that kind of money?"

"The same thing everyone else wants," she said. "To find a better life."

"There are other ways. Safer ways."

"How would you know? You're a man. You can come and go as you please. You can get a job that pays real money."

"You can get married."

"To whom? Someone who lives in this forsaken wilderness? No. This backcountry killed my mother and I refuse to let it kill me. I'm going to catch that horse and make enough money to go to San Francisco."

"What's so special about San Francisco?"

"It's civilized," she replied. "There are doctors there, and real markets and operas and stores and—"

"I get the drift," Tag said, cutting her off. "I just don't understand why you'd want to give up the sweet air and clear skies of Wyoming."

"Gee, I don't know, why, would I want to give it

up? After all, that sweet air killed my ma and turned my pa into a drunk."

"It wasn't the air that did that."

"You're right," she said. "It wasn't the air. It was love."

"Love?"

"Yeah, if my ma hadn't fallen in love with a dreamer and drifter like my pa, she'd still be alive today."

"You can't know that."

"Oh, I know it all right. Well, I'm not going to be that stupid. I refuse to let some silly emotion ruin my life. I'm going to catch this stallion and get as far from Wyoming as I can."

"So you're saying you'd never marry for love?"

"Nope. If I ever get married it will be for money. In my experience love will kill you, and I'm not ready to die."

"If you're not ready to die, then you need to go home. It's not safe in the backcountry."

"Are you saying I'm not safe here with you?"

He lifted his hat off his face and eyed her. "Honey, you're safer here with me than you'll ever be anywhere else. That's not what I meant and you know it."

"What did you mean?"

"I meant that a gal like you should leave men to do things like catch stallions. You're better off baking cookies and selling them to the general store."

"I see. I suppose you're one of these men who believe that a woman's place is strictly in the home."

"Darn right."

She stood up. "And I suppose that's because we

aren't capable of taking care of ourselves. That we're like small children and have to be protected from the big bad world."

"Of course. Today was a perfect example. If I hadn't come along you would have been trampled."

"I already told you the stallion reacted the way he did because you startled him. I can't believe how insufferable you are. How does your mother let you believe these things?"

"My ma died a few years back," he said. "She was frail and consumption took her." A stab of grief that he thought was long gone rushed through him. He placed his hat back on his head. "So, like I said, any gal should not be allowed to roam the wilderness alone. As I see it, it's a man's duty to protect what's his and, as far as I can tell, your pa's doing a poor job."

"You have no right to talk about my pa that way. You don't even know him."

"You're right. I don't know him."

"So you have no right to judge him, or me for that matter."

Tag let that statement end the conversation.

Dismay flooded him. The way he figured it, even if he tied her up and took her home, she'd just find a way back. How could you fight that?

What he needed was some time and space to figure out what was going on here. He needed to figure out why he didn't want to do the safe thing. Why he didn't want to make her go home.

* * *

Lana stared at the fire. It popped and snapped merrily. She glanced from its warmth to the sprawled-out form of Taggart Morgan.

He was clearly uncivilized and everything she despised in a man. So why did she talk to him? Why didn't she just keep her silence, stay in her crevice, and wait for him to go to sleep?

That question bothered her more than she wanted it to. Of course, he goaded her into talking. Once the words were out it would have been silly to stay inside the hidey-hole. She had forced herself to come out.

She didn't kick herself too much though. The meal had been warm and tasty. Her stomach had quit growling and she felt better. So it hadn't been too big of a mistake, but the question she had to ask herself was, what was she going to do now?

Clearly the man was more equipped to catch that horse. He had almost lassoed it this afternoon. That didn't bode well for her "ease into the herd" idea.

Lana sighed. Somehow she would just have to be quicker, more clever, and more resourceful than Taggart Morgan. Mostly she had to get off on her own. She had a feeling that this man might be capable of anything, even forcing her to go back home.

That was something she couldn't let happen. She needed the stallion. Without it her dreams of the future would be ripped away. She glanced at Taggart. His clothes were sturdy and clean. His hat and boots alone were high quality. It was clear that, unlike her, he had some resources. Maybe if she reasoned with him he would go away and leave the stallion to her.

"Mr. Morgan?"

"Call me Tag."

"All right, Tag," she said.

"What?"

"You know I have first claim to that stallion."

"The first person to capture him has claim to that beast and no other."

"Fine," she said, her temper rising at the exasperating tone of his voice. "Since I was the first one here, then I should get the first crack at capturing him."

"Are you telling me to step aside and just give you the horse?"

"I'm asking you to give me the first chance at him." Tag lifted his hat off his face. He smiled. "Honey, out here it's every man—or woman—for themselves."

"A civilized man would let a lady go first."

"As you've said, darlin', I'm far from civilized. Now go to sleep, will ya? I've got a lot of work to do tomorrow. Especially since you botched all the work I'd been doing up until today."

"Excuse me, to begin with I am not your darlin'. Secondly—"

"Go to sleep." He cut her off mid-sentence.

She could not believe that he treated her like that. "Secondly," she continued, "I am not responsible for your failure to capture that horse. You shouldn't have tried to run him down. No one is ever going to catch him that way, and we both know it."

"Are you finished?"

She narrowed her eyes at him, anger rising up from her gut. "Quite."

"Then good night."

She refused to answer him. He turned on his side and within minutes snored softly. Lana couldn't understand him. Here she was churning with anger and indignity, and he slept like a babe with nothing to worry about.

She glanced at him. He didn't even believe that she would leave. He just rolled over and expected her to do what he said. Well, his mistake.

She eased off the rock and waited to see if he woke up. She waited for what seemed like hours, but she knew must have only been moments, and moved off into the darkness.

She crested the top of the ridge and gave a little birdcall. It was her signal to her mare. Sure enough, within five minutes her horse came trotting up.

"Hello, girl, how are you? Did they treat you well?" She ran her hand along the animal's flanks and felt only smooth skin. Good, Penny had managed to hold her own among the wild mares. Much like Lana had held her own with Taggart Morgan.

She mounted and eased the mare down the opposite side of the ridge. If Tag could track her on granite, she knew there was no way she could hide her tracks from him. So she didn't even bother. No, he had said the stallion would go to the first person who captured him, and she took him at his word.

The half moon lit the ground enough so that she

could safely move through the wilderness. She had seen the stallion come into the valley from the backside and she was certain there was a pass there. Once she found the pass, she'd see where it took her.

Taggart Morgan might find her, but when he did, she'd be holding a line on that stallion.

Tag let Lana go. It was the last gentlemanly thing he would do where that gal was concerned. He wanted her in an elemental way, and that bothered him. When she had dared to ease outside the circle the campfire made, he'd wanted to jump up, grab her, and bring her back.

Primitive urges weren't unknown to him. What bothered Tag was the sure and certain knowledge that once he snagged her he may never let her go. If he did that he'd have to marry her.

That thought scared the dickens out of him. He had always been the wild one, the free one. Used to answering only to himself. He simply wasn't the family kind.

He sat up and grabbed another stick from the pile and tore into it. Then he heard her call for her horse. The call was low and whistled. If he didn't know better, he'd just heard a cardinal—except cardinals didn't call this time of night.

The gal was good, but not good enough. She'd been frozen and half-starved when she came out of that crevice. He couldn't allow that to continue.

He grinned and dug into his whittling. Soon he found himself humming the aria she had been singing.

His voice was as far from refined as hers was angelic, but the tune reminded him of the scene in the meadow. Reminded him of the moment he'd first set eyes on her.

Chapter Four

It had taken her nearly two days, but Lana finally tracked the stallion down. He had a large territory, which was why he was so well-known. Half the state of Wyoming was betting on who brought the devil in.

Lana wasn't intimidated by the idea. She knew she was closer than anyone had ever been, and she had enough stubborn determination to continue until the very end.

She heard the stallion before she saw him. He was snorting up a storm, and when she broke into the clearing she saw why.

Somehow Taggart Morgan had gotten here first. The man must have known a shortcut, or maybe he knew the territory better than she did. Or worse, he was simply a better tracker. It didn't matter. What mattered was he had managed to corral two of the stallion's mares. It was a makeshift trap, but from what she could see, it was a very efficient one.

Desperation overtook her as she watched the stallion step closer to the open gate. This would not do. She could not have that man rob her of her horse, of her very future.

She hopped off of her mare and sang for all she was worth. The sound caught the stallion's attention. Lana dug two sugar cubes out of her pocket and held them out in her open palm.

The notes of her song wafted softly, delicately, desperately over the air. The stallion stopped and turned to look at her. She let go of her mare's reins and stepped out into the sunlight. Gathering strength from the horse's reaction, she sang sweet and soft and low, offering the sugar.

The horse turned away from the trap and eyed her. She took a step back, easing away from the corral.

The stallion snorted and pawed the earth, then slowly stepped toward her. She continued to move back as the stallion sniffed the air. The song had caught his attention; now she hoped the sugar would draw him toward her. She stepped backward, he moved forward.

She started whispering sweet things, like those a mother would whisper to her child. Things like how handsome he was, how expressive his eyes and fine his face. She couldn't tell if it was the sweet talk or the sugar that drew him, but what she did know was that the horse moved toward her as surely as if she had lassoed him.

He was ten feet away and she made soft "tsking" noises with her tongue and continued to praise him in low sweet tones. At five feet away from her, she could feel the heat radiating from him, his breath a mist in the cool mountain air.

Her heartbeat sped up. Tag's warning rang through her mind. This stallion was a big animal, and she had the awful feeling that one false move would make him rear up. She kept her eyes on the horse. Death was not something she had looked forward to today, but neither was losing this animal and her future.

He stepped within two feet of her and she held out her hand, letting the sugar cubes rest in her flat palm. She held her breath as he reached out to take the sugar. A sudden cry came from behind the horse and he paused. Then another shout and the mares stormed their way out of the corral. They shot past her in a thunderous cascade of hooves.

The stallion shook his head. The spell was broken. He sniffed the air, then reared up. Lana inhaled sharply at the sight of cutting hooves flailing only feet away from her. She was frozen with shock, helpless to do anything but stand there and wait for the stallion to trample her.

Suddenly, she felt a rush of wind from the side. Then she was grabbed by two very large hands and hauled up against a huge, warm wall of man. She didn't have time to think as they hit the ground, rolling over and over.

She felt as if time had slowed. She knew they were rolling—felt the turn of earth then sky then earth again—but oddly enough she never touched anything. Instead, she was cradled in Taggart's strong arms, held tightly yet gently against his chest. Her legs entwined with his, her body pressed intimately to his.

Then, as suddenly as it had started, it stopped. She rested with her back to the ground, her face pressed into his shoulder. As best as she could tell he completely covered her, protecting her from any harm that might come their way.

It struck her that he smelled good. She took a deep breath. He smelled like pine and horse and warm male flesh. There was something elemental in the way he protected her, something warm and welcome that protected from all harm. She was safer than she had ever been in her life and she wanted the feeling to last forever.

"Are you okay?" he asked. She tilted her head up to look into his dark eyes. Up close Taggart Morgan had the face of a god: strong, well defined, and yet with eyes softened by a fringe of long thick lashes. "Lana?"

She liked the way he said her name soft and low in the back of his throat.

"Honey, are you hurt?" He ran a callused hand along her jaw.

"I don't think so," she said. He looked so concerned. It was as if he truly saw her, cared about her, maybe even wanted her.

He rested near her, not quite touching her. His body

heat traveled deep into her bones, making her feel lucid and fluid as if her bones had all melted. He studied her face as if memorizing every plane and angle that lay beneath.

"Honey," he said, shaking his head. His voice was rough as gravel and danced along her spine. He looked for all the world as if he wanted to kiss her. The thought made her hold her breath. It seemed as if he stared at her forever, drawing out her sensation of not knowing whether he was going to kiss her or not. He bent in closer and she inhaled sharply. Then he dipped his head and allowed his warm lips to touch hers.

She reveled in the scent of his skin. Enjoyed the feel of his soft mouth on hers. He pressed ever so slowly, savoring her like a longed-for sweet from the candy store.

He kissed her gently, evenly, but that wasn't exactly what she wanted. She wanted more. She put her arms around his neck and ran her fingers through his silky hair. It was cool in her fingers, soothing in the heat of their embrace. She sighed, and he captured her sigh and deepened the kiss. There, she thought. That was what she wanted.

She delighted in the taste and texture of his kiss. The emotion behind it. It was as if they were the only two people in the world and nothing mattered but the feeling of his mouth on hers.

Finally he lifted his head away from her. "Darlin,' we have to stop before I can't stop."

"What?"

"Darling, we have to stop this. I'm liking it just a bit too much."

Lana blinked. "Oh." She suddenly realized she was on her back on the cold ground. Taggart Morgan was sprawled half on her and the afternoon was quickly giving way to evening. She scrambled away from him. "What happened?"

"The stallion reared. I thought he was going to kill you so I grabbed you and rolled."

"You," she sputtered. "You let those mares out before I could catch the stallion."

"You lured him across the field," he countered. "After I spent a whole a day rounding up his mares and setting the trap."

"You let them go, knowing he would follow." Anger surged through her. "Then you grabbed me and tossed me around like a . . . like a bag of feed. Then— then you have the gall to kiss me?"

"Well now, I seem to remember that you kissed me back."

She jumped up. "I cannot believe that you are such a cad."

He rolled on his side, put his head in his hand, and grinned at her. "I'm a Morgan," he replied. "No one ever accused me of being a gentleman."

"You are incorrigible," she said.

He stood up and dusted the grass off of him with his hat. "And you lost me two days' worth of work. That means we're not square, honey. What are you going to do to fix it?"

"I don't need to fix it," she said and stepped away

from him. "You kissed me. I think that's payment enough."

"You wanted me to," he said and stepped toward her. "So I don't see that as paying at all."

"Stay away from me."

"The only way I'm going to do that is if you give up your hunt."

"I am not giving up," she said and stormed toward her mare. "I need that stallion."

He strode to her, quicker than she imagined possible, and gently turned her to him. "Why?"

"I told you why," she said and brushed him off her.

"What you told me wasn't enough to even consider being killed over."

She turned toward Tag, but walked backwards away from him. "My reasons are good enough for me and that's all that matters. If you don't like it then you can just—"

"Listen, don't go storming off. It's getting late. Let's have dinner together. You owe me that much."

She stopped in her tracks. He was right. She did owe him a dinner. She let out a whistle and her mare came trotting up. She grabbed the saddle horn and leaped onto her saddle, snagging the reins. Then she unhitched a bag of salt pork and a ration of flour from her saddle gear and tossed it at Tag. "Now we're even," she said and turned back to the entrance to the valley. "I have a stallion to catch." That said, she urged her mare into an all-out run and got as far away from Taggart Morgan as her horse's legs could carry her.

* * *

Tag watched her gallop off. She had a fine temper. He grinned. He liked that in a woman. It made life interesting. And interesting was the best word he could come up with for their encounter today.

He tossed the bag of salt pork in the air and caught it. She was one pretty woman, with a voice to make heaven weep and enough brains to keep a man guessing.

He glanced over at his ruined trap and shook his head. He had been going about this all wrong. If he wanted to catch the old beast, he needed to use a rare and special female. He needed to use Lana. "You catch more flies with honey than vinegar," he said to the air. All he had to do was convince her that they should work together.

He whistled for his mare and climbed up. The trees he had used as part of his makeshift corral would soon become part of the landscape. It wouldn't hurt to leave them.

So he headed out. He may be a better tracker than Lana was, but she seemed to be a better lure. He just had to find her and figure out how she did it.

He galloped after her.

Lana could not believe the audacity of Taggart Morgan. He had actually kissed her! How dare he think he could kiss her as if she were a common saloon girl? She might work in a saloon, but she never sold her favors. She might be desperate, but she had not yet reached that level.

Anger and excitement flowed through her, leaving her nearly breathless. The kiss aside, she had nearly gotten her hands on the stallion. She was filled with a strange energy.

Lana leaned into her mare's neck and whispered soft encouragements. They ran through a flat pass and up the side of the next mountain until they were both breathless. She pulled the horse to a slow walk.

She had to do some thinking when it came to Taggart Morgan. The man was handsome in a rugged, uncivilized way. She had felt so safe and warm in his arms that she had lost her mind. It had been a long time since she had felt safe like that. Not since she was a little girl and her mother and father had filled the house with singing and love.

That had been a long time ago. In fact, she hadn't realized she missed that feeling until this afternoon when Tag had taken her in his arms and kept her from harm.

She shook her head. She hadn't been able to sort out the feelings that flooded her. The feelings kept her from thinking straight, from concentrating on her goal. This was not good.

Lana thought she was not the only one to know Taggart Morgan was trouble. She was certain that wily old stallion knew enough to associate Taggart's smell with it. That was not good for Lana either.

Over the last few weeks, Lana had become familiar with the black stallion's territory. It contained two large watering holes. The way she figured it the stallion's herd had headed to the opposite watering hole.

With luck and good light, she'd make it to that watering hole by tomorrow afternoon.

It had taken nearly a week to get the mares to accept her and her horse onto the fringes. She was certain that the sugar she kept in her pockets had attracted the attention of the stallion.

She had to hope and pray that he didn't now associate her scent with danger.

Tag found Lana later that night. She had stopped to make camp in a small hollow. Her back was snug against the mountain and she huddled in a blanket. He threw another blanket over her. Then he coaxed the fire into a blaze and proceeded to cook himself a decent dinner. Her salt pork was good, and he added gravy to it for good measure. But he had also killed and cleaned a fat rabbit, which now roasted on a stick over the fire.

Lana was so tired she barely stirred. He wondered at her resiliency. It was obvious she was used to fending for herself, and no one else seemed to think she shouldn't. No one but him. He had the idea that she needed to be cared for, and while she was in his territory he was going to see that it happened.

He filled a plate with meat and biscuits and gravy and walked over and nudged her shoulder. She swatted him away. He kissed her cheek and she sighed. A slight smile crossed her face and it nearly undid him.

He poked her again. She jumped up and blinked at him owlishly. "Hello," he said. "I've made you dinner. Here." He shoved the plate in her hands and headed back to the other side of the fire. If he had stayed that close, he would have kissed her again.

"What?" she said and stared at the plate in her hand. Then she looked at him. "How did you get here?"

"I followed you," he said simply and proceeded to eat his own dinner. "You look cold. A good hot meal will help. Eat up."

"I had dinner."

"Whatever you ate, it wasn't nearly enough. Eat. It's good, I told you it was my ma's recipe."

She sat up and picked up the fork and took a bite. "It is good."

"Eat some rabbit. You need the fresh meat."

She did as she was told and he took pleasure in watching her. She looked soft in the firelight.

"Tell me more about yourself," Tag said.

She paused in her chewing and swallowed. "Why?"

"Why not?"

She pushed the hair out of her face and studied him while she chewed. "You go first."

"All right, I have four brothers. Trey owns the Bar M, and he and his wife, Brianna, adopted a passel full of boys off the orphan train. Then there's Matt: he's the sheriff of Amesville. His wife, Sam, is a journalist. She's in charge of Amesville's weekly newspaper. Then there's me and Shay."

"What does Shay do?"

"Matt made him go to college, so he's a lawyer."

"A lawyer and a sheriff . . . there's a lot of lawmen in your family."

"Yeah, odd coincidence."

"You don't strike me as the lawful type."

"You cut me to the quick," Tag said and put his hand over his heart, feigning pain.

"I think you'll survive it."

He sat up and grinned at her. "So I will. Now tell me about you."

She shrugged. "Not much to tell, really. My family owns a nice piece of mountain near Hunter. Pa don't work it like he used to, so I've done some stuff to help bring in money."

"What do you do? Laundry? Sewing?"

She laughed. The sound was soft and musical and made his heart hurt. "No. There isn't much money in that. If you must know, I found a job in the Buckhorn Saloon."

He felt the roar inside him, making him want to stand and fight. Instead, he urged it down. "What do you do in a saloon?" He sounded pretty cool. That was good because he didn't feel cool. He'd been inside his share of saloons and none of them were good places.

"I work there."

Horrified, he swallowed something down the wrong way. Food stuck in his throat and he erupted into a coughing fit so bad it made his eyes water. There was no way his Lana worked in a saloon.

"Are you okay?" She jumped up and came over and pounded him on the back.

He nodded, but had trouble catching his breath. "Swallowed something wrong," he choked out and grabbed a canteen full of water. A few large swigs and he could breathe again.

She shook her head and went back to her side of the fire. "I suppose I shocked you."

"No," he squeaked.

She grinned and his heart melted. "Yes, I shocked you. That's okay, it's not what you think."

"What do I think?"

"Well, whatever you're thinking it's not that," she replied rather tartly. "Like I said, my father hasn't been well and we needed the extra money."

"So you got a job in the saloon?" He could barely say the words.

"I got a job singing and playing the piano," she qualified.

He wasn't sure he heard her right. "You just sing and play the piano?"

"Yep," she said with a firm nod. "That's what I do."

"What does your father say about that?"

She blew out a breath and pushed her half-finished plate toward the fire. "He likes to reminisce about the time he first saw my ma. She was on stage at the New York Met and he swears it was love at first sight."

"So he doesn't say anything about you singing at the saloon."

"I sing at church too," she replied rather haughtily. "But they don't pay and there aren't any tips."

"So it's all about money."

"When you are poor it's always about money."

"Darlin', only certain kinds of women work in saloons."

"That's right," she said. "Poor women."

He shook his head. "It ain't right."

"What isn't right?"

"You aren't the saloon kind."

"If singing in the saloon earns enough money to feed us through the winter, then I'm the saloon kind." She studied him. Her big eyes were clear and soft. "Does that bother you?"

Chapter Five

"I can't believe that your pa lets you work in a saloon." When Lana didn't reply, he pressed her. "What does your pa do to put food on the table?"

"Pa's not been well since my ma died."

"So you're the one taking care of him?"

"Mostly."

Tag had all he could do not to pound something. She seemed so small and dainty to have the care of a family on her shoulders. "Do you have problems with the men inside the saloon?"

She shrugged and wrapped herself back in the blankets. "Sometimes they get the wrong idea but not often, and Hal, the bartender, usually takes care of anyone who gets too close."

"Thank God for Hal," Tag muttered. Silence wove between them, each lost in their own thoughts. Sick father or not, Tag figured he just might have to stran-

58

gle him. What kind of sod let his only daughter sing in a saloon? Especially when she was young and pretty. Not to mention when she had a voice that could coax Satan himself out of hell.

"You want that money so you can quit singing in the saloon?"

"Not exactly," she said. "I want the money so that I can take pa and move to San Francisco."

"Why San Francisco?"

"It's as far away from Wyoming as I can get."

"What's wrong with Wyoming?"

"Wyoming is where my ma died," she said, her tone soft and quiet. "Wyoming is where my life fell apart." She looked at him with her big pixie eyes. "I have yet to find anything worthwhile in Wyoming."

For some odd reason her words hurt Tag. Wyoming was where he belonged. Where his family was. Where he wanted to live.

"What about the mountains?" he asked. "They don't have anything like the Tetons in San Francisco."

"They are beautiful, but San Francisco has the ocean."

"What about the stallion? I thought he was what you wanted."

"He's a means to an end," she admitted. "He'll help me get out of this place and my whole life will be different. More than anything, I want my life to be different."

"And you think that's what moving to San Francisco will do?"

"Yes, I do." She looked at him and he saw fierce determination in her eyes.

"Good luck with that."

"Thanks." She stood up and picked up her plate. "I'll do the dishes this time." She took his plate as well and moved off to the creek.

Tag leaned back against the mountain and studied the night sky.

He needed to capture that stallion to complete his own herd. So he was going to do it. If he had to, he would use Lana to bring the stallion in.

Lana washed the dishes using sand from the bottom of the creek that spilled down the side of the mountain. She had been so tired when she stopped for the night that she hadn't bothered to do much more than care for her mare and roll up in her blanket.

Both the meal and Tag were a total surprise. It had been years since she had someone cook for her. It made her feel almost decadent.

She puzzled over how easy they were around each other. It wasn't awkward at all, not even after the kiss they had shared.

She touched her lips as she remembered the emotion in their simple embrace. She knew that kissing was fun. She'd seen enough of it at the saloon, and the men and women always smiled after, but she had never realized how wonderful it was.

She wondered if she now had the same strange smile that came over their faces. She bent to peer at her reflection in the water, but the moon was covered by clouds and all she could see was a shadow the shape of her head.

She sighed. Human emotions were strange. She knew from watching the men and women interacting in the saloon that a gal had only one thing going for her in this world, and that was to make the best match possible. Life wasn't about love, or even attraction. It was about looking out for yourself and doing the best that you could with the assets you had.

Taggart's strong, handsome face came to mind. He had the most compassionate eyes. He looked at her like she was an angel. She found she liked it. That look and his kiss seemed to cut through all her bravado, all her reasons for being out here.

She frowned. It wasn't good to feel this way, and she knew it. Her mother had given up all her dreams to follow an uncivilized man into the wilds. Lana had vowed at an early age never to do the same.

Heart-stopping kisses or no, she was going to do the sensible thing. She was going to capture the stallion and leave Wyoming. For all she knew, Tag was a drifter with no prospects, and prospects were all that mattered in this cold world.

"Lana," Tag called. "Hurry up, there's a storm brewing."

Lana shook away her thoughts and finished the dishes just as the first drop of rain hit her shoulders. She scurried back to camp to find Tag putting the finishing touches on a small shelter.

"What is that?" she asked, cautiously eyeing the size of the tarp.

"It's what's going to keep us dry," he said and held out his hand. The rain had started to come down in earnest. "I'd suggest you get under it."

"There's barely enough room for you," she protested. "I don't think we'll both fit."

"We'll fit," he promised and crawled in. He had placed blankets on the ground and put their saddles as pillows.

Lana's heart raced when he lifted a blanket and patted the ground beside him. She wasn't even close to being ready to share a bed with this man. It was too intimate and he was too, well, too male. "I really don't think so."

"Come on," he said and patted the ground again. "I won't bite."

"What about the horses?" She stalled.

"They're fine, I hobbled them and threw an extra tarp over them. Besides, they're good mares, they know when to get in out of the rain."

She cringed at his pointed words. The rain soaked her father's coat and ran down her face. Still, she hesitated. The man was big and warm and gentle and she just didn't trust her own emotions in this situation. Anything could happen, and that thought more than anything else bothered her.

Tag rolled his eyes and laid his head back on his saddle. "Suit yourself, but don't blame me if you catch a cold and have to go home."

That caused her to move. If she caught a cold, the stallion would be Tag's for sure. She dove into the shelter and wiggled onto the blanket beside him. Then she took off her jacket and shook the rain off it. Placing the jacket over the blanket to dry, she realized that Tag had a very male grin on his face.

"What?"

"I knew that would get you," he replied.

Arrogant man. She ground her teeth and refused to comment. Instead, she pulled out the small calico bag where she kept her brush and unbraided her hair. He didn't speak at all while she brushed. Her hair was nearly waist-long and so fine it tended to fly away a lot. She remembered that her mother had the same kind of hair and her father had loved to play with it, calling it strands of pure moonlight.

"I like that tune," he said.

She jumped. "What tune?"

"The tune you were humming."

"Oh." She hadn't realized she was humming. She thought about it a moment and realized she was humming the lullaby her mother used to sing whenever she brushed Lana's hair.

"What song is that?"

"It's a lullaby," she said. "One my mother used to sing me to sleep with."

"It's pretty. Sing me some of the words."

She felt the heat of a blush rush up her cheeks. It was too intimate to be sitting in a small shelter in the middle of the wilderness with this man and singing a song. It was as if the magic of the forest wound around them, binding them together.

"Go on, you must know the words."

She brushed her hair into a curtain between them and sang a verse of the song.

"More."

She blew out a breath and continued, her fingers flying as she braided her hair into one long single braid. She finished the song just as she flipped her braid back behind her. Her hair had been wet from the rain, but was so fine that it dried quickly.

"That was beautiful," he said. The truth in his words shone through his eyes. "You are beautiful."

She felt a blush rush up her neck and into her face. "Thanks," she said and decided it was best to pretend she was alone. "Good night."

"Good night."

She slid down under the blanket and turned away from him. It didn't help that she had to practically lie up against him. She didn't want to touch him. It brought back too many memories of their kiss. It was better if she just ignored him. She closed her eyes and listened to the rain hit the tarp above them.

"My ma loved to sing," Tag said, breaking the silence. Lana opened her eyes, but did not turn over.

"Ma used to sing these little kids' songs and clap and dance. We thought she was so beautiful." He sounded almost wistful. "Then, when it was late at night and we couldn't sleep, we would take a blanket and come sit with her by the fire."

"Where was your pa?"

"He was usually out with some sick calf," he replied. "Ma would be waiting by the fire, brushing her hair. We would ask her to sing for us and she would smile and sing some silly tune."

She heard the sorrow in his tone, the sadness and longing. "How long has your ma been gone?"

"Just a few years," he said. "But I can still hear her singing."

Lana smiled. "I can still hear my ma too," she said. "Sometimes I sing with her."

Silence greeted her comment. Embarrassed, she said, "I suppose that sounds silly."

"No," he replied.

She glanced over her shoulder to see him lying with his hands under his head, gazing at the top of the tarp. She was certain he didn't really see it. He was seeing the past. Her heart squeezed. She did the same thing sometimes.

She turned on her side to face him. "You miss her." It was more a statement than a question.

"Yeah," he said. "I miss her." He looked at Lana. "She used to say that I was the lucky one. Being born in the middle made me strong. I'm not so sure she was right."

Lana frowned. "What does that mean? Of course you're strong."

"I don't always do the right thing," he said with a small shrug.

She shook her head. "Who does? I'd like to meet that person and ask them how they manage to do it."

He laughed at that and she felt better. It was good to see him laugh. It felt so right being in this shelter with Taggart Morgan. It made her almost wish things were different.

"Can I ask you something?"

"Sure," he replied.

"What do you do for a living?"

"I work on my brother's ranch, taking care of horses mostly."

She swallowed. Her idea of him was right. He had nothing. "You live with your brother?"

"Yeah, Trey, he's the one with the new wife and their boys."

"Boys? But you said they were newly married?"

"They adopted them," he said.

"Oh." She lay back down. "Why?"

"The boys were on the orphan train and were adopted out by a selfish group of miners looking for slave labor."

"And?"

"And my brother and his new wife rescued them."

"How did they know about them?"

"One of the boys was Brianna's brother."

"Goodness—"

"He was only ten."

"Poor baby."

"Trey figured he'd never have a family."

She smiled. "He has one now."

"Do you want kids?" Tag asked. "I mean, when you go to San Francisco."

"I'd have to have a husband first," she said. "But kids would not be out of the question if I knew I could keep them safe." The thought of children made her heart warm. She'd always wanted babies. Lots and lots of babies to coo to and sing with.

"But you want kids, right?"

"Yes, I want kids."

"How many?"

"Why?"

"Just curious."

"I guess four would be the most. How about you?"

"I'm not sure," he said and shrugged. "I've never seen myself as the marrying kind."

"Then are you always going to live with your brother?"

"Naw, I'll have my own ranch."

"Really?"

"When I bring in the stallion, I'll have enough to buy my own place."

Lana felt a stab of guilt. She hadn't considered what he might want the stallion for. She hadn't wanted to know. It made it too personal. "Is that why you're here? To earn enough for a ranch?"

He didn't look at her. He stared up at the tarp. "That's part of it," he said with a casual shrug. "That and my reputation."

"What reputation?"

"Some consider me the only man who can bring that horse in. They say I'm that good."

"I see," she said and turned onto her back. There wasn't much room in that position. Her whole side touched his and, while he was warm and the feeling was infinitely pleasant, she knew she should turn away. So she did.

"Good night."

"Good night," he answered yet again.

She lay there and listened to his breathing, highly aware that he didn't sleep. The idea that he wasn't the marrying kind played through her mind.

"You think you'll always live alone?" she suddenly asked.

"I don't know. Maybe."

"Won't you get lonely?"

"Naw, I'll bring my nephews over."

She let that go for a while, but kept thinking on what he said. Truthfully, she didn't believe him. He was just too good of a kisser to never marry.

"Don't you want someone to cook and clean for you? Someone to make your new ranch a home?"

Tag glanced at her, curious. She was fishing and he wondered why. He thought he'd play along. He inched over just enough to let his shoulder touch hers. "Maybe. If the right gal came along, I might change my mind."

"Do you have anyone in mind?"

"Well, there is this one gal," he said. He felt her hold her breath. "You know, back in Amesville."

She let out her breath and he raised an eyebrow. It seemed to bother her that he might have a gal. That made things just a bit more interesting.

"What's she like?"

"Well, for starters, she doesn't sing in a saloon." He glanced over and caught a frown on her face.

"I suppose she teaches Sunday school," Lana said rather snottily.

"Yep, loves kids too."

"I suppose she's also stunningly beautiful."

"Looks like an angel," Tag said. "You want to know the best part?"

"What's that?"

"She does everything I say."

"Sounds like she's an idiot," Lana muttered and pulled the blanket tighter to her.

Tag grinned. "What was that?"

"Nothing," Lana said.

Victorious, Tag inched a fraction closer, enjoying the way she kept scooting away. He was pretty sure he was annoying her. It was like teasing the girls when he used to go to school. "Yep, it may be good to have a woman who does whatever I say without so much as a single bit of back talk."

"Hmmph," Lana said and pushed him away. "Get over on your side, you're crowding me."

Taggart did as she asked and hid his grin.

"So what's her name?" Lana asked.

"What?" Fear spiked through him.

"What's her name?" Lana turned to face him. "She does have a name, doesn't she?"

He swallowed. It was difficult to think when she looked at him with those beautiful eyes. What made it worse was that she was tucked up beside him. It didn't matter that they were both fully clothed and had separate blankets.

She raised one delicate eyebrow. "Have you forgotten your own angel's name?"

"No."

"Okay," she said as if he were suddenly either very stupid or dead drunk. "Then what is her name?"

"Sally," he spit out. "Sally Sly."

"What kind of silly name is that?"

"Now there's no reason to make fun of a gal's name. Besides, once I get my ranch she'll become Sally Morgan. That's not a bad name. In fact, I sort of like that name."

She narrowed her eyes at him as if judging whether or not he was lying. "What if she doesn't like the name?"

Affronted, he looked at her. "Why wouldn't she like that name?"

Lana blew out a breath and flopped back down. "I don't know. Knowing your angel, she'll probably love it."

"Of course she will," he said, relieved not to be caught. "Sally Morgan is a much better name than, say, Lana Morgan. Don't you think?"

"Oh, much," she muttered.

"You do realize, of course, that if you get married you'll have to change your name."

"So?"

"So, I don't think it's something a gal considers when she's doing the picking. Do you?"

"A gal's got other things to consider besides a name," she said tartly.

"Oh, like what?"

"Like how much money a man has, how stable his

work is, and whether or not he can keep her and her children safe."

"Hmmm, I didn't think you were the type."

"What type?"

"The type that would marry a man for his money."

Chapter Six

"I'm whatever type I want to be," she said.

"That's saying a lot."

"Well, I suppose you're the type that would marry the prettiest gal who came along regardless of whether you loved her or not."

"Maybe," he said with a shrug. "Or maybe I'm just not the marrying type."

"You mean you're not the type to fall in love."

"Maybe I'm not," he said simply. "What's it to you anyway?"

That gave her pause and Tag chalked up one for his side.

"Oh, go away," she grumbled.

"Can't, it's raining, remember? Besides, this is my tarp."

Tag let the sound of the gently falling rain surround them. A soft sweet pleasure filled him. The warmth and weight of her body next to his made him feel protective. He kind of liked the feeling.

Tag put his hands behind his head and reveled in the darkness of night, the scent of fresh rain, and the warm sweet perfume of the woman beside him. The rain muffled night sounds. A section of Lana's hair had escaped the braid and teased the side of his face.

Lana's breathing evened out and he knew that she was asleep. That meant she was comfortable around him.

Tag frowned. There was a sense of trust building between them. A trust that couldn't go any farther than the backcountry. That made him a cad.

He knew he couldn't live with that. He might not be a gentleman, but Morgans were born with a strong sense of honor. What he was about to do didn't sit well with that. He wrestled with various ideas of how to fix the situation.

He supposed he could take her straight home, then come back and stick to his original plan. No, he knew that she would just show up back here. She was desperate for the money. Well, shoot, he had money.

That was the answer. He'd give her what she needed. A sense of pride filled him. It felt good to know he could help her. In fact, he could picture her throwing herself at him. Maybe even covering him with kisses. Yeah, maybe he could get a couple more of those soul-stirring kisses from her before she left.

That thought gave him pause. If he gave her the money, she would leave. He glanced at her. He hadn't thought about never seeing her again. He didn't like the idea. Heck, he didn't like the pain that gathered in the pit of his stomach when he thought about it.

Well, shoot, he thought. Maybe he could keep her around for just a few more days. He didn't see how it could hurt.

Lana was up at the first light of dawn. For some reason she had slept like a baby. It was the first time in years. When she woke up, Tag had his arm thrown over her waist and had hauled her up against his chest. It felt wonderful for just the smallest of guilty moments. Then she knew she had to move away.

She was not going to make the same mistake her mother made. She was not going to fall in love with an uncivilized man. No matter how much she might want to. As far as she could tell it always ended in heartache.

Maybe this Sally Sly could make it work. Maybe she had the stuff to put up with Tag always bullying people into doing what he wanted.

One thing Lana knew for sure, she would never allow Taggart Morgan to bully her. She'd simply start singing and he would do everything she asked. She smiled. What a sight that would be. She pictured him practically drooling as he fell into her hands.

"What is that you're singing?"

Lana paused. Guilt shot through her. It was as if he could hear her thoughts. "I was singing?"

"Yes," he said, his voice gravely from sleep. "I think it was the same song you sang to the stallion yesterday."

"Oh," she said and packed her things.

"What is the name of that song?"

"It's called, 'My True Love'."

"I like it."

She swallowed. She might just be in trouble. Her mother always warned her not to sing that song to any man but her intended. She had claimed it had the magic to bind a man's heart forever.

"Something about it gets me right here," he said and patted his chest right over his heart.

Panic raced through her. She swallowed it down. "It's just a song," she muttered and snatched up her bag, then retrieved her saddle.

"What are you cooking for breakfast?"

"Who said anything about breakfast?" she replied and headed off to saddle her mare.

Tag was out of the blankets and beside her before she took her next breath. For a big man he moved quieter and quicker than anyone she had ever seen. She glanced up as his hand wrapped around her elbow.

"I've cooked for you twice. Don't you think it's time you feed me?"

"If I remember correctly, you force-fed me both times. I never asked you to follow me or cook for me."

"Please." He said the word soft and low. It danced along her skin and made her traitorous knees go weak.

"I have a stallion to catch."

"I want to talk to you about that."

"You are not talking me out of this," she said and shook off his hand. "I am catching that stallion."

"Okay," he said. "I was thinking that working

against each other wasn't helping either of us reach our goal. So, I wanted to know what you thought about working together."

Suspicious, she narrowed her eyes. "You mean you want me to catch him for you."

"No," he said and pulled the saddle out of her hands. "I was thinking about this last night. You want that two grand, right?"

"What do you mean?"

"I mean, that reward is for whoever brings that stallion in, but you aren't going to keep the stallion, right? After all, you're going to be moving to San Francisco. I doubt that the big city is the right place for a magnificent horse. Especially one we haven't proven can be broke yet."

"So?"

"So, I want the stallion to start a horse ranch. I want to keep him here in Wyoming."

"Then catch him."

"Well, now hear me out. We stand a better chance of catching him together. I say we work together. When we have him and have tamed him a bit, then you take him into town and collect the bet."

"What about you?"

"That's the beauty of it. When you get ready to leave, you give me the stallion for my ranch."

"Just give him to you."

"Yes. After all, you'll have the two grand. It would be greedy to ask for more. All I want is the horse."

"All you want is the horse?"

"Yep."

"I get the reward and then give you the horse."

"Yep."

Indecisive, she hugged her waist. "I need to think on this."

"Fine," he said with a grin. "I'll stoke the fire, you make us breakfast."

Lana blew out a long breath and watched him walk away with her saddle. It seemed he had out-maneuvered her again.

They worked well together. Tag enjoyed watching her eyes light up when he suggested something she liked. Then she would take it a bit farther and he would smile. They thought a lot alike.

It didn't hurt that she smelled good. Like soft sunshine and clean mountain rain. Her hair glowed in sunlight or moonlight and her eyes twinkled. She hummed when she set about a task. The best part was she was almost always singing and she didn't even seem to realize it.

He was certain he made the right choice keeping her around for a few days. Heck, they may even catch the old beast.

Tag chopped down aspens and Lana took her small ax and cut the smaller branches off. Soon they had a fair-sized pile. They planned on making another corral, only this time the bait would be Lana and her sugar cubes.

Since Lana appeared to be accepted by the group, Tag was certain it was the one lure the old beast couldn't refuse.

For good measure, the mares would be inside too. Once they got the old man inside, Tag would slip a bridle over the stallion's head. Then all hell would break loose.

They worked until noon in a small bottlenecked canyon. When they stopped for lunch they had a sturdy barrier across both ends of the canyon. There was a large gate on either side.

They ate only cold biscuits and jerky. In the fall the sun went down quick, and they both knew the urgency of daylight.

When Tag put the finishing touches on the trap, he did a final walk around the corral. Lana walked with him, taking two steps for every one of his. He slowed down to match her pace, but kept his eye on the fencing.

"It looks good," she said. Pride was in her voice.

"I think it might actually work," Tag admitted. "This was a good spot. How did you know about it?"

"I found this the second day I was out hunting. I know he comes this way almost every evening. It's how they get to their watering hole."

"Clever." Tag smiled at Lana. She smiled back and he had the sudden urge to grab her and kiss her. He doubted she would let him this time.

The sun was low in the sky and the wild horses would come soon.

They hobbled their mares inside the makeshift corral to prevent them from running off with the stallion. Lana had suggested it. She worried that her mare was getting a bit too friendly with him.

Lana situated herself on an overhang to the right of the first gate. There was a big enough space between that and the mountain so that she could scramble behind it should anything go wrong. It was the safest spot Tag could have her in and still use her.

The mares grazed near the second gate and Tag knew he had to be fast. He would have to close both gates and bridle the stallion before anything bad happened. It would be close.

Adrenaline surged through him. He was up for the fight. The way he figured it, the wily old beast would suspect a trap. He would have to move both quickly and cautiously if he were going to accomplish his goal.

A thunderous sound could be heard in the distance. "Ready?" Tag asked.

"Ready."

"Are you going to sing?"

"Should I?"

"Yeah, I think that's how they identify you. Let the old boy get a good whiff of you, then hold out the sugar. While you're distracting him, I'll lasso him. Then climb up that rock outcropping fast because he's going to get mad."

"How mad?"

"Fighting mad," Tag said. "Mad enough to try and kill us with those hooves of his, and trust me, honey, he could do it."

"Then I'll get out of the way fast."

"That's my girl," he said and patted her shoulder. "I'm counting on you to stay out of the way."

She frowned. "I'm not stupid."

He grinned. "No, just headstrong and reckless."

"Do you have a problem with that?"

"No, Ma'am."

"Good, now get to your spot before they just run on by."

The thunder grew louder.

Tag raced to the far gate. He took up position near the edge, partially hidden by a large tree branch they had left the leaves on.

The thunder grew until a dust cloud could be seen coming around the bend of the valley. It was the mares. The stallion drove them relentlessly.

They came snorting and running around the bend and straight into the corral. Sunshine lifted her head in alarm, but Lana's mare, God bless her, kept eating calmly as if being stampeded was something that happened to her every day. She kept Sunshine calm.

Lana sat perfectly still. The mares slowed as they passed her. The corral barrier was nearly invisible in the dusk. The horses reacted with fear and uncertainty. They rolled their eyes, kicked out, and whinnied their distress as they milled around Lana.

Her heartbeat sped up. The animals had accepted her earlier that week, but things were different now. She hadn't been part of the group for a few days. What if they rejected her?

She decided to hum a calming tune. The lead mare turned her head in Lana's direction. She rolled her eyes and snorted. Lana knew it was now or never. If the lead female did not accept her, she would be lost.

There would be no hope that the stallion would even enter the corral.

Lana turned the hum into a song. It was a sweet, soothing lullaby her mother sang to her when she was a child. Now, whenever Lana was afraid, she sang the tune. It always kept the monsters at bay.

The lead female came over to inspect Lana. Time seemed to stand still. The loud noise of distressed horses milling about her dimmed as Lana concentrated on keeping up her quiet song. The lead female snuffled her, snorted, then pushed her on the shoulder.

Lana moved back. The horse nudged her again. Lana's heart threatened to jump out of her throat. She held her ground this time. Then the mare nudged Lana's right side. It dawned on Lana what the horse wanted. She kept the sugar cubes in the right pocket of her father's coat.

She smiled and pulled out one sugar cube. Holding out a flat palm, she let the mare sniff it, then gently take it. The lead mare then nodded her big head and turned her attention back to the fearful harem. Lana breathed a sigh of relief. She was once again accepted.

Now all she had to worry about was the stallion.

Tag let out the breath he had held when he saw the big bay mare confront Lana. He had been tense and ready to save her if things went wrong. Seeing her safe had him breathing better.

A scream filled the night air. Tag saw the stallion just outside the corral. The massive animal was up on his hind legs. His strong front legs and powerful hooves slashed the air.

The stallion screamed again and the big bay mare answered him. The old beast stopped outside the gate. He slashed the air one more time, then came down to sniff and snort at the corral walls.

"Come on," Tag whispered under his breath. "Come on in and rescue your ladies."

The stallion snorted and pawed the ground. Tag held perfectly still. The beast called to his mares. They milled about. He called again. The lead mare nudged her foal back toward the entrance to the corral.

Tag could feel their goal slipping out of his grasp. The stallion was very clever. He refused to enter the corral and now was sweet-talking his mares to come out.

Tag wavered. He could close the gate now and he would have the mares and foals, but not his stallion. Or he could leave the gate open and gamble that the mares would call the stallion in to save them.

He had to make a choice and he had to make it quick. The stallion called again. The bay and her foal ran back through the gate. Tag glanced over. Lana looked at him with widened eyes. Tag signaled to her that it was all right.

The mare and her foal ran behind the stallion. The old beast called again, but the other mares did not come. Their fear had overridden their instinct to obey the stallion's call.

The stallion wove back and forth in front of the opening, calling and pawing.

"Come on, boy," Tag whispered. "You're going to have to come in to save them. Come on."

The stallion seemed to make up his mind. He screamed, slashed the air with his front hooves, and came down flying. He tore through the gate and into the herd. In a blink of an eye he was behind them, herding them with a wave of his magnificent head.

Excitement rushed through Tag. They had him. All they had to do now was follow the plan. He signaled Lana. She sang, soft and low, catching the maddened animal's attention. He herded the mares past her. They rushed back through the open gate, but the stallion did not follow. Instead, he stopped in front of Lana. He pawed the ground, but she didn't move. He snorted and moved closer. Tag could hear her sweet-talk the old boy as she held out her hand.

That was his cue. He swiftly and silently stepped out from his hiding spot and quickly twirled his lasso. Just a few steps closer and he would have the old man.

The stallion lowered his head as if to take the sugar from Lana's hand. It was Tag's perfect opportunity. With an expert flick of his wrist, he tossed the lasso.

At the last moment the stallion jerked aside. He must have seen movement from the corner of his eye. When the rope fell short at his feet, he rolled his eyes, slashed the air, and screamed.

Lana scrambled up her rock.

Tag was all business now. It was just him and the old beast. He pulled in his rope. The stallion threatened him. Tag kept his eyes on the stallion's dangerous hooves and once again twirled the lasso.

The stallion reared, narrowly missing Tag. He thought he heard Lana call his name, but he didn't respond. This was life or death. He needed all his skills to get the job done, and get it done he would.

The stallion reared again, hooves flashing. Tag let go of the lasso. It flew through the air and fell into place around the stallion's neck. Tag dug in his heels and held onto the rope for all he was worth.

It took everything he had. The stallion reared and screamed and pulled. He tried to drag Tag one way, then the other, but Tag held on. He could feel his muscles being pushed to their limits.

The old beast bucked again. Taggart leaped to the side, but deflected a blow with his shoulder. Pain shot through him and he could no longer hold on. The stallion ran out of the corral.

Taggart held his shoulder and watched the old beast taunt him from outside the corral. The stallion leaped and twisted and slipped right out of the rope. Then he reared, screamed his victory, and ran off to his mares.

Taggart kicked the dirt. Anger and frustration welled up and mixed with the pain that ran through his arm.

"Are you all right?" Lana asked.

"Yeah," Tag managed to get out.

"Did you break your arm?"

Taggart wiggled his fingers and bent his arm. "No, he just glanced me."

"It was strong enough to make you let go."

"It's just bruised," he muttered and grabbed his hat off the ground. "Come on, we might as well make camp. There's nothing more we can do tonight."

"We might as well make camp right here," she said.

"The horses are already hobbled and there's plenty of cut wood for the fire."

Taggart looked around. "All that work. Gone." He glanced at her. "It's the second time I've built a corral."

She raised a winged eyebrow. "Well, then it would seem to me that the corral concept does not work. So we'll just have to come up with something else."

"Right," Tag said and slammed his hat on his head. "We'll come up with something else."

Chapter Seven

Frustrated with himself, Tag picked up a thin stick, sat down, and whipped out his knife. Whittling was what he did when he needed to think. He concentrated on his stick. A cool night breeze flowed through the pass. It smelled of snow. Tag knew that wasn't a good thing. If it started snowing, they could be trapped in three to four feet of the white stuff in a matter of hours. It was okay for him, he'd done it before, but it would not be good for the little songbird.

"What are you making?"

He looked up to see her standing in front of him, her head cocked. "It's a bird."

"Really?" She stepped closer and sat down beside him. He could smell her sweet scent, feel the heat radiating from her body. He realized that he liked the feel of her next to him. He liked it a lot. He was in deep trouble.

Taggart swallowed. "Yeah, well, not yet but it will be."

"Can I watch?"

"Sure," he said. But it was tough. He usually just carved small animals and birds. He didn't think about the process. No one ever watched. He simply let his fingers develop the piece of wood.

He worked in silence for a while. It was one of the toughest things he'd ever done.

"Do you do a lot of this?" she asked.

He jumped, startled, and sliced his thumb. "Ow!"

"Oh, no. I'm sorry. Is it bad?"

He shoved the offended digit into his mouth. "It's fine."

"Let me see it."

"I said it was fine."

She simply frowned and held out her hand. Tag withdrew his thumb and gave her his hand. Her hands were warm and soft and competent. Her head bent over his hand.

"You cut it pretty deep," she said.

"I'm sure it's fine." He thought he could feel her heart in the palm that held his hand. Then he was certain he could feel his. The two beats sped up as he looked into her beautiful eyes.

"Let me fix it."

He didn't say anything. He couldn't say anything. He was dumbstruck. She pressed on his thumb. Her fine hair blew across his cheek, silky and inviting. Her sweet breath blew on the cut as she examined it.

"I think pressure and a bandage will do the trick," she said. "But I can stitch it if it doesn't."

"Stitch it?!"

She glanced up. "What's wrong with that? I'm a very good seamstress. I made this outfit I'm wearing."

"I'm not saying that you aren't. I just have . . . well . . . a thing about needles."

"Have you had stitches before?"

"No, Matt did. I was there when his wife sewed him up after a gunshot wound, and well, let's just say the world went dark."

She grinned then, the moonlight dancing in her eyes. "You fainted."

"I didn't say that."

"You didn't have to." Her grin grew. "Here, hold this tight and I'll go get something for a bandage."

He pressed his thumb. The last thing he needed was for her to think he needed stitches. So, he willed the bleeding to stop. By the time she got back from retrieving the small roll of cloth, his thumb was white from the pressure.

"You don't have to hold it that tight." She took his hand again. The feel of her hands on his soothed him. He was able to breathe a little.

"I really think it will be all right without stitches," he said.

She didn't look at him. "Do you have any whiskey?"

The question made him break out in a sweat. "Will it hurt that bad?"

She glanced up. "It's to clean the wound with, silly."

"Oh." He told himself to breathe. He had to tell himself, for he was getting dizzy. "Yeah, there's a small flask in my saddlebag."

She pressed a small cloth to the wound. "Hold this on here and I'll go get it."

Tag watched her walk away. Then he lifted the cloth and really looked at the slice. He kept his knives razor-sharp. This time he had split his thumb through a couple of layers of skin and muscle. But since the bone wasn't showing, as far as he was concerned it wasn't that bad.

Still, it was nice the way she worried over it. Then he realized he shouldn't want her to worry over him. He put the cloth back on and squeezed it tight. He needed to get her out of the backcountry and away from him.

"I think once we get it clean and bandaged, it will be fine," she said, pulling the flask out of his bag.

"Great."

She hunkered down beside him. "You might not think this next part is so great."

"I've cleaned a wound before."

She went to work, removing the small patch, opening the flask, then pouring a small amount of whiskey on the wound.

Pain shot up his arm as it felt like the whiskey was burning a hole clear through his thumb. He bit the side of his cheek to keep from hollering. Tears welled up in his eyes and he prayed she wouldn't ever do that again.

She glanced up at him. "Sorry."

"No problem," he squeaked.

She ducked her head, but he swore she smiled. She cut another thick patch of cloth, then wound a length of it around his thumb. She finished by tying it neatly.

Then she did the most remarkable thing. She raised his thumb to her mouth and kissed it. It was a small gesture, like the one his mother used to do whenever he had gotten himself hurt.

"There, all better," she said. Her gaze connected with his and heat shot down his spine. Before he knew what he was doing, she was in his arms and they were kissing.

The kiss was deep and passionate. It spoke of the longing he knew he shouldn't feel, but was afraid he already was feeling.

Lana melted in his arms, her kiss taking as much as he was giving. He desperately wanted to turn things up. They were alone in the dark. There wasn't anyone here to protest.

Instead, he softened the kiss.

She couldn't stay. He couldn't make her stay—it was just too dangerous. He pulled away and planted small kisses on her forehead, her eyes, and her temples.

Holding the back of his neck firmly, she pulled him to her mouth. This time she feasted as much as he had feasted. She wanted him as much as he wanted her.

He knew it in the way she kissed. In the way her hands wandered over his shoulders. In the way she melted against him.

He swore he could die and go to heaven, as he had just experienced the sweetest thing on the earth.

He pulled away and held her close. She clung to him. Their hearts raced in unison and he looked up at the clear, star-filled sky.

"I don't know why I did that," she admitted. "It just seemed like the thing to do. I didn't mean to . . . well, to . . ."

"To what?"

"To lead you on."

"You're leading me on?"

"Aren't I?" she asked. "After all, after we catch the stallion, you'll be going back to your ranch, probably with your Sally and I'll be moving to San Francisco."

He had to swallow the question that burst in his brain. Oh, right. Sally was his pretend fiancée. "Um, listen," he said. "I have to be honest with you."

She pulled away from his chest and looked at him. "You haven't been honest?"

"Not completely," he answered.

"I'm listening."

He cleared his throat. "Um, there is no Sally."

She blinked at him. "No Sally?"

"No, I made her up."

"Why would you do that?"

"Because I didn't want you to feel sorry for me."

"Why would I feel sorry for you?"

He shrugged. "Because I didn't have a gal."

"I see." She leaned her head back down on his chest. He held her against him. His hands caressed the cotton of her shirtsleeves. She was so small and wonderful in his arms. It was a perfect fit.

"Well," she said, breaking into his thoughts. "I don't want you to think I just go around kissing men. I don't, you know."

"I know," he said. "It's not exactly your fault."

"What does that mean?"

"I mean, we're out here alone. You've had a couple of rough days."

"So you're saying I kissed you out of . . . what? Loneliness?"

"No," he said. "I'm saying you kissed me because I'm irresistible."

"What?!"

"We're alone in the dark and you find me attractive. There was no stopping yourself."

"Why you arrogant—"

He grabbed her hands before she could pummel him. He knew his grin reached from Wyoming to Montana, but still he couldn't help himself. "If you're waiting for me to apologize for my actions, then you've got a long wait ahead of you."

"You, sir, are no gentleman."

"I never said I was," he agreed. "But I think that's what you like best about me."

She gasped. "I never said I liked you. Now let me go."

He let go of her immediately, but it bothered him

to hear her denounce him. After that kiss and all they'd been through. Clearly, she was just being stubborn.

She scrambled up from the ground and brushed off her cute bottom, then huffed over to her side of the fire.

Silence played around them as he returned to his whittling and she took out her brush and prepared her hair for the night.

"Tag," she said.

"Yes?"

"Did you really make up the part about Sally Sly?"

"Yep. Stupid, I know."

"Can I ask you something else?"

"Shoot."

"Would you ever move to San Francisco?"

He shook his head. "Nope. Listen. That is the sweet sound of a Rocky Mountain night. The very air you breathe is kissed by God. That's what my pa taught me and I believe he was right. There is no finer place to raise horses and children. Besides, my family is here, my heart is here. Like that stallion you want, I belong here."

She sighed and tied a ribbon around the end of her braid. "I wish I belonged somewhere."

He barely heard the words, but they lodged in his heart. "Honey, you could belong here, if you chose to."

"No, I can't. Wyoming is too hard on my father. It would be best if I could take him away to a place with less memories."

"Like San Francisco."

"Yes," she said softly, "like San Francisco. Plus, in San Francisco I can sing in the opera house."

"Is that your dream? To sing in an opera house?"

She laughed then, a sad sound with no musical tone. "I don't have a dream. I've been too busy caring for my father to really dream."

Tag wanted to strangle the man. If she weren't sitting across from him, he would grab his horse and hunt Lana's father down. Seriously. Something needed to be done with him. "My ma said everyone should have a dream. It's what makes life worth living. Otherwise you're just surviving, and that makes us little better than a blade of grass."

"I guess I'm a pretty big blade of grass."

"If you could have any wish in the world, what would it be?"

She glanced at him. "It would be that my father found a new reason to live."

"What if you could only have a wish for yourself?"

"For myself?"

"Yes, let's say your father suddenly becomes happy. What would you wish for yourself?"

She frowned and tapped the tip of her brush against her chin. "What would I wish for myself."

"Yes. Would you wish for love?"

She laughed then. The sound sent chills down his spine. "No, I would never wish for love."

"Why not?"

"Love is what took my mother from the glamour of New York to an early grave in nowhere Wyoming. I swore I would never ever let that happen to me."

Curious, Tag had to ask. "Was she unhappy?"

"No," Lana said suddenly. "Now that you ask, I can honestly say I never saw her unhappy a day of my life. Even when we slept in a wagon in pouring-down rain, she made a big adventure out of it, and when we barely had enough cornmeal to make journey cake, she used potatoes and made up some story about how potato cakes were all the rage in New York."

"Sounds like your mother didn't have any regrets."

Lana stared at the fire. "No, she didn't." She glanced back at Tag. "But I do."

"What do you regret?"

"I regret losing my ma at such an early age. I saw her waste away, half starved, her beautiful voice silenced by consumption. If we had lived in New York, there would have been doctors who would have helped."

"Think about it, Lana. Your ma left New York willingly. She must have had a bigger dream than singing in the Met. Maybe that dream was you."

Tag wasn't sure, but he thought he saw tears roll down her cheeks. She wiped her face and lay down on her bedroll. "Good night, Tag."

"Good night." He returned to work on the figure he was carving. His thumb throbbed from the cut, but the bleeding had stopped and Lana had padded it enough so he could continue whittling. His bruised shoulder protested as he worked, but he ignored it. He had bigger problems, like the coming snow and letting his songbird go.

"Tag?"

"Yeah?"

"Can a dream be simple?"

"A dream can be anything."

"Then I dream of a big warm house where my children can feel safe and a place where my pa would be happy." She paused. "That's not too bad of a dream, is it?"

"No, that's not bad at all."

"Tag?"

"Yeah?"

"If you did find a gal to marry, what would she be like?"

"She'd be like you, Lana." He thought he heard her sniff.

"Would she kiss like me?"

"Yeah," he said. "I'd wish for a gal that kissed like you."

"Thanks." She turned on her side and drew the covers over her.

Tag was left alone with the cold realization that tomorrow he had to send her home. After that he would never see her again.

Lana woke up early the next morning, feeling strangely sad. She sat up and stretched. Tag was already up. His bedroll was packed and his gear ready to go. She blinked and stood, throwing off her blankets. Had she overslept?

She glanced at the sky. The first pink of dawn was streaking through. It was early. Her next thought had her heart racing and her back up. Was he going to try and sneak off after the stallion himself?

"What are you doing?" she asked.

Taggart turned toward her. "I'm packing up. There's a big storm coming."

She glanced at the sky. There were only thin clouds covering the deep early blue. "It doesn't look like a storm."

Tag continued to pack up. "Take a long whiff and tell me what you smell."

Lana wrapped her arms around her waist and filled her lungs with clean mountain air. "It smells like . . . like snow."

"Exactly." Tag nodded toward the sky. "In a few hours we could be sliding around in snow up to your waist. I suggest we break camp and go home."

"No," she said and raised her chin.

"I mean it," Tag said. "I'm breaking camp and we're going home."

Lana hugged herself tight. A whisper of danger blew down her spine, but she refused to give in to the urgency in Tag's movements. "I'm staying."

He stopped and glared at her. "You're going home if I have to tie you up and take you home myself."

"No," she said again. "I'm too close to getting the stallion. I will not give up now."

"Look," Tag said. "If this is about the money, I've got more than that saved up. I'll give you the two grand if it will get you to go home."

Lana gasped. "Who do you think you are?" she said, fury sparkling in her eyes. "I never took any money for kisses in the saloon and I'm not starting with you." She turned on her heel and stormed toward the saddle-bags.

Tag was beside her in a flash. He grabbed her arm in his gentle grip and stopped her. "I'm sorry if you thought I was paying you for your favors. I'm not, and frankly I think you know that. Now quit being stubborn. Go home with me now and I'll pay you two grand for the help you've given me so far."

"I don't take charity," she said and pulled out of his grip. The man was going to drive her crazy. She had a feeling it wasn't just the scent of the snow driving him to make her leave. "This isn't about the snow, is it?" she asked. "This is about that kiss. You can't work with me anymore because of the way I led you on. Fine. I can do this by myself."

Tag threw his arms up in the air. "You are the most stubborn, hardheaded, mule-like woman I have ever met."

"At least that's better than you. You're a self-serving, wild man who doesn't even have a girlfriend. It's no wonder the way you act around a lady."

"A lady?!" He took a step toward her. Lana took a step back. The look in his eyes had her regretting her last statements. He looked like he would take her apart.

"I don't see any ladies here," he said, his fists clenched, his body in a gunfighter's stance. "Ladies don't run around the backcountry alone or work in saloons."

"Well!" Lana said. "It appears to me that we have nothing left to say to each other."

"So it appears."

"Good."

"Great."

Lana burned with anger and embarrassment. She wanted to clock something. Worse, she wanted to throw her arms around Tag and kiss away the hurt that flickered in his eyes when she mentioned his lack of a woman.

She tossed her saddle blankets over her mare's back, then put up the saddle. Guilt wracked her and burned the anger out. Tag had been nothing but kind to her. He was right, she hadn't acted like a lady.

She turned to apologize, but he was gone.

Chapter Eight

Taggart was madder than a wet hen. He felt it was better he left before he did something outrageous. Like tie Lana up and take her back to Amesville. Matt would understand if he threw her in jail.

Samantha would have a fit.

Then he would have two stubborn women after him. Ugh. He wasn't so sure he'd survive that, and he knew for certain that Matt would just hang back and grin while the women exacted their revenge.

As far as Tag was concerned there was only one option left. He had to capture that old beast before Lana did. It was the only way to get her to go home where it was safe.

He kicked Sunshine into climbing faster. The scent of snow was getting closer and he hoped to reach the horses' watering hole before the storm did. With any luck the stallion and his family of mares and foals would have the same idea.

Lana heard the stallion scream before she reached the top of the ridge. Panic surged through her as she urged her mare over the ridge. Had someone else gotten to the stallion first?

What she saw when she looked down at the watering hole from the top of the ridge made her heart stop.

The stallion's hind legs were covered in tangled netting. He was half in and half out of a hole deep enough to cause him harm. Scattered grasses and brush must have covered the netting that hid the hole. The stallion must have stepped right into the horrible trap.

It broke Lana's heart to see the proud and beautiful animal screaming and struggling. The mares had scattered to the stumpy pines that surrounded the hole. They whinnied their distress. The horses were making enough noise to attract the attention of predators. She wouldn't be surprised to see a mountain lion nearby.

If she was going to save the animal, she had better work fast. She urged her mare forward. They started down the side of the short ridge that shielded the water hole.

"Lana, stop!"

Lana pulled her mare to a halt and listened. She could have sworn she heard her name among the chaotic sound of horses in distress. Her horse moved restlessly under her.

"Hello?"

"Lana." This time she knew for certain she heard it. It sounded like Tag, only weak.

"Taggart?"

"Be careful." He paused and she strained to hear him. "Booby-trapped."

"Tag, where are you?"

"Lana, listen to me. I need you . . . I need you to . . . to do exactly what I say."

"Taggart, tell me where you are."

"Lana, promise me you'll do what I tell you." His voice was weaker and she knew the panic inside her was growing. It was clear Tag was in some kind of trouble, but so was the stallion. She glanced at the struggling animal. His struggles had slowed. Foam flecked off his sides and his nostrils flared, he was tiring.

"Lana!"

She turned back to the sound of Taggart's voice. "The stallion is hurt. I need to rescue him."

"Don't!"

"Why not?"

"Please, just trust me, Lana. I need you to promise that you will do everything I say."

Lana took in the desperation in his voice. She glanced at the stallion one last time, then sighed. "I promise."

"Good." He sounded relieved. "Now, get off your horse and hobble her so that she can't go too far."

"Wh—"

"Don't ask why," he said. "Trust me."

She dismounted and hobbled her mare, then turned back to the sound of his voice. "Now what?"

"Do you still have that knife?"

"Yes," she said and pulled it out of her boot.

"Good, now I need you to listen to me carefully. This entire area is rigged with booby traps. I need you to try to follow my exact path. I rode into this area so there should be signs of a shoed horse."

She looked around, taking small steps in a straight line. She saw a fresh set of horse tracks. These hooves had the distinct mark of metal. "I found it."

"Good, now slowly come toward me."

"Okay." Lana's heartbeat sped up. The stallion still struggled in the background, breaking her heart. But the sound of Tag's voice drew her. He was in trouble, and he was counting on her to help him out. She owed him that much. He'd done nothing but try to take care of her. No one had done that since her mother died.

After she had followed the tracks a hundred yards, she looked up and scanned the horizon. "Where are you?"

Tag waved his hand. Lana gasped. He was pinned to the ground by his mare. Like the stallion she had walked into a trap. A second hole had broken the animal's legs. Blood oozed from her forelocks.

Lana's first reaction was to rush to Tag's side. She took two steps.

"Stop!"

Lana froze.

"You have to go slow, honey. I have no idea how

many traps are lying around out here. The last thing I need is for you to get hurt."

Lana swallowed her panic and concern and nodded. "I understand."

"Be careful."

"I will." She eased herself forward, watching every step and remaining inside Tag's tracks. "Who would do such a thing?" Lana asked.

"Someone after two grand," Tag replied. "Someone who didn't care how he earned it."

"That someone should be shot," Lana muttered to herself.

She looked up. She was only a few yards away. Tag looked pale as death. His horse had ceased her struggle, breathing heavily from the pain.

"Hang on Tag, I'm almost there."

"Good girl," he said.

She reached the animal and rushed around to Tag. The horse she couldn't help, but Taggart she could. He was pinned at his waist. She hunkered down beside him so that he didn't have to use too much energy to talk to her.

"I knew you would come," he said through gritted teeth.

"You knew?"

"I knew nothing would keep you away from your quest . . . not me, not snow, not even an offer of two grand."

Lana blinked. He made her sound crazy. She wasn't crazy, just determined. Now was not the time to argue the point. The wind chose that moment to kick up.

Cold rushed past her, stinging her nose and cheeks. "What do I need to do first?" she said.

"I need you to shoot my mare."

"What?!"

"She's in pain, honey. If we try to move her off me, we'll just put her through more pain. It's best if we put her out first."

Lana glanced at the big dark eyes of his mare. She was a beautiful animal with long lashes. The mare closed her eyes and panted. It was clear that she was in deep agony. Lana's heart broke. She held back a sob. "Where's the gun?"

He pointed to his right. "I pulled it out when she started going down, but the impact of the fall made it fly out of my hand."

Lana saw the gun lying a yard away at the base of an old twisted pine. She stood up.

"Watch your step," Tag warned. I don't know what ground is safe."

"Only a madman would do this. Who knows how many animals have been caught?"

"Hurry."

Lana picked up the gun and retraced her steps. No one said a word as she cocked the gun and with trembling hands put it close to the mare's head. She took a breath and tried to pull the trigger. Her breakfast rose into her throat. She pulled the gun away and looked at Tag. "I can't. I just can't." She sobbed.

Tag dropped his head to the ground and closed his eyes. "It's okay. We'll think of something else."

"You both gots a heart o'gold now, don't ya?"

Lana jumped at the sound of a strange voice. She whipped around to see Sam Gooding. He looked down at them from atop his horse, his gun drawn.

"Mr. Gooding, thank goodness you're here. Help me get Tag out from under his horse."

"Like he said, yer gonna hafta kill her first," Sam said and spit a long stream of tobacco juice.

"I can't." Lana glanced at the mare. It was clear she was struggling.

"Lana, who is it? I can't see over the horse."

"It's Sam Gooding," Lana said. "He's going to help us."

"Good," Tag said and closed his eyes. "Good." He looked so pale and tired. Lana knew it was imperative that they do something, and fast. For on top of everything, the storm Tag predicted had arrived. Huge flakes fell from the sky like white lace.

"We have to do something now," Lana said with desperation. "Or they'll both end up dead."

Sam leaned against his saddle horn, cocked his pistol and shot the mare in the head. Lana gasped as the bullet whizzed by her and into the animal. The mare no longer struggled. Her mouth went slack.

She whirled on Sam. "How could you?"

"Just bein' practical," he said and spit again. "Just like them traps she stepped into. I laid those out to protect myself from the others who thought they was good enough to capture the old boy. I couldn't have them ruining my foolproof trap, now could I?"

"You—You're the one who put these horrid holes in the earth?"

"Yeah, clever wasn't it?" he said. "Just like gettin' rid of you. I can't have ya hanging around while I work that stallion now, can I?"

Lana's heart leapt into her throat. She tightened her hand around the cocked gun she held behind her back. "What are you saying?"

Sam pointed the gun toward Taggart. "I'm saying that as much as I regret it, I'm gonna have to kill you two. Now put your gun down."

"No!" she commanded. "Look, we'll let you have the stallion. Just let us go."

"Can't do that," he said. "You know about my traps. We both know it ain't exactly ethical, an' I can't have any witnesses or they might not give me that there two grand. Now drop your weapon."

"Lana," Tag said. "Do what he says."

"Yeah, do what I say or I'll have to shoot you first." He moved his gun until it pointed at her.

Lana swallowed hard and moved without thinking. She swung around and tossed the gun into Taggart's hand. He fired before she would have had time to aim.

The bullet hit its mark and Sam Gooding dropped off his horse. Lana moved up beside him. The shot had entered his shoulder, leaving his left arm useless. He opened his eyes and frowned.

"Now that wasn't at all nice."

"It was practical," she said.

"Except'n ya got the wrong arm," he replied and lifted his right arm. She saw the gun out of the corner of her eye. In a flash, she kicked it out of his reach.

His gun was flung out of his hand as his arm went limp.

"What do you think you're doing?" Sam asked.

"I'm stopping you," she said. Then she turned and raced toward Taggart.

He sat up and pointed the gun at Gooding. "Tie him with the rope from my saddle."

Lana grabbed the rope and tied Sam's hands. The man scowled at her and his gaze made her skin crawl. "You don't deserve that stallion," she said.

"I'm bleeding," he whined. "Aren't you going to help me?"

"I'll help you after I help Taggart," she replied and ran back to where Tag lay. He rested in the snow with the gun still pointed in Sam's direction. "Tell me what to do."

"We need to get my mare off my legs," he said through clenched teeth.

"Hang on." The wind kicked up, swirling the flakes around them, stinging her nose and cheeks with cold.

"You're bleeding." He pointed to her left arm.

"It's just a scratch," she said. She studied the heavy body of the dead animal. "I just have to figure how to do it."

"You'll need leverage," he said. "Find a long thick branch. It'll help you lift her."

Lana glanced around. She spotted a thick branch lying beside one of the scrubby pines. It was gnarled and not very long, but it was the only practical choice. She needed to move Tag, and she needed to move him now.

She grabbed the branch and hauled it over to where Tag lay. He helped her place the branch firmly under the mare's spine. Then with all her might she pushed down on her end of the branch.

"It's working," Tag said with gritted teeth. "Keep pushing, honey, I can see my calves."

"Hurry, Tag, I can't keep this up much longer," Lana said. Her muscles strained and pain shot through her.

"You need more leverage," Tag said. He sat up and helped her adjust the pole so that the end was farther under the mare. "Now put all your body weight on it."

Lana strained with all her might, throwing her body into pushing the branch down.

"I can see my knees. Keep pushing."

Lana pushed down harder when a terrifying crack filled the air. She glanced at the branch. It had started to give way in the middle. She could see a gash in the wood that ran from one side to a few inches from the other. "Hurry, Tag," Lana said through gritted teeth. "Hurry, the pole's breaking."

She heard him wiggling and sliding beside her, but she dared not take her concentration off the branch. Sweat ran off her forehead and into her eyes, her heart pounded, and her arms and legs ached. There was another crack from the branch and she felt it weaken. "It's going, Tag! Get out!"

"I'm almost there," he said through gritted teeth.

"Almost isn't any good," Lana said as the crack widened and the horse's body began to drop. "It's going!"

The branch broke, throwing her headfirst onto the snow-covered ground. The impact took her breath away and she lay there for a moment, trying to breathe.

"Lana? Are you okay?"

Lana rolled over and studied the gray sky and blowing snow. "Yeah, I'm okay," she said. "Did you get out?"

"Yeah," Tag said. "I'm free."

Lana sat up and blinked at him. He sat beside the mare's body and rubbed his legs. "Are they broken?"

"No," Tag said, but there was a look of pain on his face. "She threw me before she went down. I tried to roll out of the way, but there was nowhere safe to go."

Lana got up, brushed the snow out of her face, and went over to Tag. She hunkered down beside him. "Can I help you?"

"Sure."

She massaged his ankles, his calves, and up to his knees. It just wasn't proper to go any farther. Her hands hovered at his knees and she looked up. Tag watched her with a strange intensity. "What?" she asked.

He shook his head as if to shake off a mood. "Nothing."

"Is that better?"

"Yeah, thanks." He bent his legs and Lana held out her hands. He took hold and attempted to stand. He wavered a bit and Lana put his arm around her shoulders and steadied him with her hands on his chest. She could feel the warmth of his big body. His pulse beat slow and heavy against her gloved palms. He smelled like fresh snow, wet leather, and man.

"Think you can walk?"

"Yeah, I'm just stiff."

"Let's backtrack to my mare," Lana said. "We know that path is safe. I saw an outcropping on the other side of the ridge. That would be a good place to hunker down for the night. At the very least our backs would be out of the storm."

Tag nodded. He was clearly in pain as he struggled to take steps with her. Lana eyed her dark mare in the distance. She barely made out her form in the blowing snow. It was simply too far for Tag to walk. She glanced around.

Sam Gooding's gelding had wandered to the stand of pines and turned his back to the trees. "Stay here," she said and pulled away.

"What?"

"Trust me," she said, throwing his words back at him.

He looked like he was about to protest, so she turned away. In a few long strides, she was back at the horse. She picked up the biggest piece of the thick branch. Then she carefully moved to where Sam's gelding stood. With any luck, she would walk the same path he did. In any case, she tested the path in front of her with the stick.

The gelding snorted when he saw her approach. "It's okay," she said softly. "I have a present for you." She reached into her pocket and pulled out a sugar cube. "Here boy." The gelding took the gift from her flat-palmed hand. "Good, good," she said. She grabbed the reins and the horse shook his head. "I know," she said and stroked his muzzle. "I'm scared of the snow too, but I promise if you come with me, I'll get us some shelter. Okay?"

The animal eyed her with caution, but followed behind. Reins firmly in one hand and the stick in the other, Lana slowly made her way through the snow. It was almost four inches deep and still coming down.

"I don't know if that was the smartest or the stupidest thing you've ever done," Tag said.

"I'm not hurt, so it was the smartest," Lana said.

"Hey, that's my horse," Sam said. He struggled to get up.

"So?" Lana said matter-of-factly.

"So, I need him," Sam struggled to stand. "Darn it. I'm in pain here."

"So is Taggart and so is that stallion," she said. "You should have thought about that before you dug all these traps." She took the bedroll off of his saddle, unfurled the blanket, and tossed it over him. "Now, just sit still and if you're lucky the bleeding will slow down."

Taggart gave her a sidelong look. She ignored it. "Do you think you can mount?"

"I'll do my best."

Tag leaned on Lana as he threw one leg over the horse and settled into the saddle. His face was solemn and Lana noticed the fine lines of pain etching his mouth and around his eyes. "Good job," she encouraged. "Now let's get to my mare and find some shelter.

Tag didn't respond. Lana glanced up to see him concentrating on getting rid of the pain. She had to get him to shelter and soon. He was hurting from the cold and lack of proper circulation. If that turned into frostbite, he might lose his toes or worse.

It seemed like hours before they reached her mare. The snow wasn't more than half an inch deeper, and at the rate it was falling it would be three feet deep in a few hours. She could never say Tag hadn't warned her about the snow, she thought, but if she had gone home Tag would have died. Her heart squeezed at the thought.

She took a deep breath of the cold air. She needed to keep a clear head. Everyone was counting on her. There was no room for strange emotions.

Lana unhobbled and mounted her mare, tying the gelding's reins to her saddle horn. With determination, she headed back up over the ridge. She could only pray the outcropping was where she thought it was.

The horse's movements jarred Tag, causing pain to shoot up his thighs and into his spine. He held on for his life as they eased through blowing snow. He'd been stupid. That's how he'd ended up in this painful situation. If he hadn't been in such an all-fired hurry to get to the stallion first, he would have noticed the traps.

That kind of thing never escaped him. But this morning his mind had been on other things. He'd wanted to shake Lana for not listening, and he'd wanted to kiss her because, well, because she needed kissing and he was the one to do it. He'd been the reckless one this morning and he'd lost a good horse because of it.

"We're almost there," Lana said, cutting into his internal berating.

He hung on as they trotted toward the rocky side of the ridge. His teeth hurt from clenching, but it was a good distraction from the pain in his legs.

"Tag?"

"Yeah."

"Are you doing okay?"

"Peachy."

Silence followed them into the shadows. It was mid-afternoon and the only way you could tell in all the snow was the lightness of the gray sky. Tag knew in a few hours the sun would set and then even the snow would be invisible in the darkness.

"We're here," Lana said and stopped the animals. She dismounted and walked over to Tag. "Let me help you."

"I'm fine," he said and tried to lift his leg back over the horse, but his body wasn't having any of that. He almost fell on top of Lana. She was stronger than she looked and managed to stay on her feet.

"I gotcha," she said and put his arm over her shoulder. Tag struggled to walk on wooden legs. The pins and needles he had originally felt were gone. His legs were numb and he knew that wasn't a good sign.

"Duck," she said. They walked into a sheltered outcropping. The ground under it was damp at the opening, but dry toward the back. Rocks and fine orange-red dirt covered the floor. Lana helped him sit down near the back. "Try to get some feeling back in your legs," she said with a look of deep concern in her eyes. "I'm going to take care of the horses and the gear."

Tag stopped her. "What about Gooding?"

"After I get you settled, I'll go back for him."

"Are you okay with that?"

"Sure," she said and looked down at the hole the bullet had made when it slashed through her father's coat. "He's tied up and I'll have your gun. I hate to bring him here, but I can't just leave him out there to die."

"You're right," he said. "But after word gets out about the way he treated these horses, he'll be lucky a lynch mob doesn't string him up."

"Can't say as I blame them," she said. "He deserves the same fate as your mare." She stood up. "It won't take long to get the camp started and your feet warmed. By then the storm should have taken most of the fight out of him. I'll be all right."

"Okay." Tag watched her duck out of the stone overhang. She was little, but she was brave and bold and beautiful, and shoot . . . he was already half in love with her.

Chapter Nine

The cold, relentless wind howled outside the small shelter. Lana built a fire and helped Taggart take off his boots. His feet were very pale, but showed no sign of frostbite. She melted enough snow to get a pan full of water. Then she heated a saddle blanket near the fire and they worked until Taggart regained feeling in his feet.

Lana knew it hurt. She offered Tag some whiskey and he took it willingly. Then she wrapped him up in the warmed blanket.

The small fire snapped and popped and Lana fed it bits of twigs to keep it going. She glanced at Taggart. He slept now, but the color had returned to his face.

It was time she went back out there. The snow still fell in reckless abandon outside and Sam was probably getting cold. She knew his gunshot wound wasn't very bad, but the cold had turned violent.

Then she thought she heard the faint scream of the stallion.

The horse would die if it remained trapped overnight. Some mountain lion, the wild horse's most feared enemy, would be lured in by the stallion's screams.

Lana's heart broke. She glanced at Tag again. He was warm and safe. Their horses were covered with blankets and sheltered on two sides by the cliff. As far as Lana was concerned, going out there was the only thing she had left undone.

She stuffed a pistol into her waistband, pulled her sturdy gloves on, and grabbed the rope from her saddle to form a makeshift bridle. She couldn't leave the stallion out there alone. Somehow she'd have to get both Sam Gooding and the stallion.

Lana shrugged down deeper into her father's coat and headed out into the late evening light. She would have to walk. It wasn't safe to take her mare into the valley. This was a journey she would have to make alone.

The wind howled at the top of the ridge, obscuring her view. Her cheeks were half frozen and her booted feet numb. She ignored the discomfort. Now came the hard part. She held a long thick branch out in front of her and swept the snow for traps. It was nearly six inches deep now and she had no idea how many traps were between her and Sam Gooding. The new snow obliterated their earlier trail.

It took longer than she wanted to get down to where

Tag's horse had gone down. "Mr. Gooding?" she called.

There was no answer and she frowned. The gun in her waistband was little comfort in the dark with a wounded villain. "Mr. Gooding?" She stopped a few feet from the mound that was Tag's mare.

Sam was nowhere to be found. Lana swallowed hard. What had happened to him? Had she been gone that long?

"Mr. Gooding!" she called. The only reply was the scream of the stallion. Lana whirled around.

The small clearing where the watering hole lay was just below her. Perhaps Sam had gotten up and gone after the stallion. There was a lot of area between her and the horse. She had no idea how many traps waited in between. She dared not take a step without testing it with the stick.

It took her what seemed forever to make her way down the mountainside. Finally, she broke out of the stand of trees that ringed the watering hole. It was deathly quiet, except for the howling of the wind. Lana's heart dropped into her throat. Had Sam gotten to the stallion after all?

Taggart woke to an awful silence and sat up. The fire had died down and Lana was nowhere in sight. Panic rose in his stomach. He could hear the howl of the wind and little else.

"Lana?"

There was no answer. He pulled socks on his now pink feet and tried to stand. He was sore and wobbly, but his legs were steady under him. With one hand on the roof of the small shelter, he took the few steps to the edge of the overhang. "Lana?" he called out toward the horses.

No reply.

Tag muttered a curse under his breath. She had gone back for Sam Gooding and not returned yet. He glanced out as the storm raged on around the shelter. The snow was a foot deep and had begun to build up in drifts.

Taggart growled with frustration and the inability to do anything. He was still weak and sore. Even if he managed to pull his boots on and go out into the storm, there was little chance he would find her now. Darkness had fallen.

"Lana!" He shouted her name into the howling wind. It did no good. Frustrated, Tag grabbed his boots and tugged them on his swollen feet. Pain shot up his legs, but he ignored it. He grabbed his jacket and slipped his arms in the sleeves, then he reached for his pistol. It was gone.

Good. At least she had the sense to take a weapon with her. He gritted his teeth and watched the darkness for any sign of her. He knew there was no way he could stay in the shelter. Not with Sam Gooding out there. Not if there was a chance she was lying face first in a snowdrift, slowly freezing to death.

Tag wiped his hands over his face. Since he'd been in Lana's company, he'd badly bruised his shoulder, cut his thumb and darn near broken both legs. If he went out in this storm he would more than likely end up dead. Tag shrugged. Even though she frustrated, confounded, and goaded him at every opportunity, he liked her. He blew out a deep breath and pushed into the storm.

Then Lana heard a faint yet tired snort. She pushed forward, her stick checking her path inch by inch. Suddenly in front of her she made out the form of the stallion amongst the falling snow.

He was half in and half out of what looked like a six-to-eight foot deep hole. Three of his legs were tangled in rope netting and the more he struggled the more tangled he got. Lana looked around. Sam was nowhere to be seen. It was just her and the magnificent stallion.

He watched her with large wary eyes, huffed, puffed and struggled, then was still. Lana knew he was close to the end. Through cracked lips, she sang a bit of the lullaby she had sung to him before. His ears perked up.

She worked her way toward him. She knew this was dangerous. He had almost killed her before. He could kill her now and there was no one around to save her.

Lana was on a rescue mission. The reward money was insignificant now. Her only goal was to free the stallion from the death trap that held him.

"Hello there," she said in a gentle tone. The stallion snorted. He struggled to get out of the pit, but the more he struggled the more he got tangled in the netting and the deeper into the pit he fell.

Lana reached into her pocket and pulled out her last

sugar cube. "It's okay," she said and held out her hand. "I'm here to help you."

The stallion flared his nostrils, but she continued to step forward. He struggled toward her, then rested. She could hear his heavy panting. She reached out and stroked his neck. He did not protest. Encouraged, she held out the sugar cube and continued talking to him in a soothing voice. He pushed her shoulder with his nose, then took the sugar she offered.

"That's it, take it. I'm your friend and I'm going to help you." She stroked his neck down to his front shoulders. He tolerated her attention. "You are so beautiful." The snow whirled around them, but Lana concentrated on the horse. "Okay, now I'm going to have to put a bridle on you," she explained and took out the rope bridle. "It's for your own good. You have to trust me. This is the only way I can help you."

She slipped the rope over his ears and into his mouth. He snorted and sneezed three times, but he accepted the strange device. "Good," she said and patted him. "Now, I'm going to get you out of that net."

He rolled his eyes and watched her closely as she pulled out her knife and cut away at the netting that held his legs.

"I knew it wasn't me you came back for."

Lana froze at the sound of Sam's voice. She turned slowly to see him standing a few feet away. His hands were untied. One held the shoulder where Tag had shot him and the other held a gun. It was pointed right at Lana.

She glanced at the pistol in her belt.

"Come on," he said with disdain. "We both know you're not fast enough, girlie."

Lana swallowed hard. The stallion struggled beside her.

"Put your knife down and move away from the horse."

Lana did as she was told.

"Put your hands up. Keep them up." Sam moved in closer to the stallion as Lana stepped back. The gun did not waver. "Thanks for putting the bridle on him," Sam said with a wicked grin and grabbed the rope with his free hand. "Saves me the trouble of beating him into submission."

"You are an evil man."

Sam laughed. "Naw, just single-minded. Right now I'm concentrating on that two grand."

The stallion must have sensed the tension in the air. His struggles became stronger. Sam cursed as the bridle was jerked out of his hand. He slammed his fist into the horse's nose.

The stallion screamed. Lana leaped forward, reaching for the gun. Her feet slid out from under her in the snow, but just before she went down she was able to knock the gun away from Sam. The motion caused him to lose his footing and slide into the pit that held the stallion.

Lana's knife had freed the stallion's front leg and the animal fell back into the pit. Screaming filled the air. Lana covered her ears at the sound of horse and man in a fight to the death. It seemed to go on and on forever.

Then there was silence. An awful silence. Lana didn't want to look up, but she was so cold and numb she knew she had to move.

"Lana?"

She lifted her head. A large dark figure of a man loomed in the nearby darkness. "Tag?"

"Lana, are you all right?"

She thought she heard him curse as she struggled to get up. He was beside her in an instant and they clung to each other. The embrace was warm and desperate. He wiped the snow from her face.

"I'm okay," she said through numb teeth.

"I heard a shot."

"I knocked the gun away from Sam," she said into his chest. She clung to him with all her might. "When I did it, he fell into the pit with the stallion." She sobbed. "It was horrible."

"It's okay," Tag said and held her against him. "It's okay."

"I think he's dead."

"Stay here," he said and gave her a squeeze. "I'll take care of everything."

"But your legs—"

"Are fine. Don't worry." He let her go and moved closer to the hole. Lana hugged her waist and wiped the tears off her frozen cheeks.

"Be careful."

Tag held out his hand as if to say he would. She watched as he moved slowly to the edge of the hole. He hunkered down and spoke in soft sounds. After what seemed like forever he slowly reached down, and when he stood, he had the reins in his hands.

The stallion watched him warily, but listened as Tag gently pulled him forward. Tag's muscles bunched and his legs splayed as he slowly but carefully hauled the stallion out of the pit.

The animal struggled to get its front hooves up on the edge. Then with a lot of coaxing from Tag, he kicked his way up and out of the hole. The netting was now hanging off his haunches.

Tag whispered something to the animal and carefully took out a knife. Then, with quick even strokes, he cut the remaining netting away. The stallion shook it off with a fierce kick.

Tag held onto the bridle with all his might. "Come on, big guy," he said. "Settle down."

Lana sang the lullaby again. The sound seemed to soothe the beast. "Come on, boy," she sang. "Come back to camp with us."

The stallion studied her with liquid eyes. His breathing was labored and his hide covered in lather. He shook his head and settled down. After having fought the netting for hours, it seemed at least for now he had no more fight in him.

"Come on, old boy," Tag soothed. "Come on, we'll get you out of the cold and to some oats. I promise."

"How did you find me?" Lana whispered as Tag led the stallion out.

"I followed your trail in the snow."

It was what they were doing now, following snowy

footprints. It was the only way they could be sure not to fall into another trap.

"What about Sam?"

"I told you from the start," Tag said, his tone low and very serious. "A wild stallion is a dangerous animal. If it weren't for the bridle and his exhaustion, I doubt we'd have him following along this easy."

Lana glanced at the horse. The animal's proud head was bent. She had been naive to think she could have pulled him out of the hole. She swallowed hard. It could have been her at the bottom of the pit.

She didn't say another word.

Taggart stirred the thick pot of beans and bacon. The fire snapped and popped and warmed the tiny shelter. His boots were standing side by side near the fire to dry.

He glanced up at Lana. She looked exhausted.

"That smells good," she said.

"I found the parboiled beans in your saddlebag and figured we needed something warm and substantial."

"We forgot your saddle," Lana said and laid her head back against the rock wall as if it were a big tragedy.

"Hey," Tag said, gentling his tone. "You did great today. What's a saddle when I owe you my life?"

Lana didn't open her eyes and Tag thought he saw a tear forming on her lashes. It rolled down the side of her cheek and his heart melted. He reached for her and drew her into his arms.

She rested her head against his chest. He pulled the

stiff leather gloves off her hands and rubbed them between his palms. Then he undid her jacket, spread the wet leather out on the ground near his boots, and drew her closer to him.

He rubbed her arms and brushed the hair out of her face. "It's okay," he said and wiped the tears off her face with his sleeve. "You can cry now. You did a good job. You were fearless and bold, and we're safe here in this shelter."

Lana hid her face in his shirt. "Sam Gooding died in that pit." She shuddered. "It could have been me."

"Hey," he said and took her chin in his palm so that he could see her beautiful eyes. "You can't look at it that way. You have to think of how brave you were. You saved my life and yours and the life of that stallion. That man was a predator. There is no reasoning with someone who set traps like that."

"Oh, those traps were horrible." She sniffed. "It makes me so mad to think that he set them on purpose."

"That's it, honey, you get mad."

"The man was an animal." She tucked her arms around her waist and leaned against Tag.

"Yes, he was worse than an animal. He chose to do the things he did." Tag held her close and rubbed her arms. She had started to warm next to him. Luckily, the tears seemed to help unthaw her face. Her cheeks and nose were bright red from the wind and the cold, but there was no sign of frostbite.

"We captured the stallion," she said.

"That we did," he said and kissed the top of her head. "That we did."

Lana closed her eyes and in a moment fell into a deep sleep. Tag lifted her up and laid her on her blanket. He pulled off her wet boots and rubbed some color back into her feet. Then he took the warmed blanket and tucked her in. It would be a while before she woke, but that was fine.

He didn't know very many men who could have done what she did today. She had earned his respect, and that was no easy thing to do.

Lana slept for nearly two days while the storm raged outside. She got up only long enough to check on the horses and eat more of Tag's bean soup. Then she crawled back into her blankets.

At some point, Tag had moved his blankets over and doubled the warmth with his body heat. She was too exhausted to protest. If she were honest with herself, she'd admit that she liked snuggling in the safety of his arms.

"Lana, honey, wake up."

She opened her eyes when Taggart pushed her shoulder. "What is it?" she said and sat up straight, instantly awake and on the lookout for danger.

"Listen," Tag said.

Lana listened but heard nothing. In fact, it was unearthly quiet. She glanced at Tag. He was completely dressed. "The storm's over," she concluded.

He smiled. "Yeah. It looks like there's about four

feet of snow. Do you think your mare could move through it?"

Lana rubbed her eyes and stretched. "Yes, she's good in the snow." She glanced at Tag. "You'll have to take the gelding. We have no idea how good his footing is."

"Why don't you eat the last of the beans and start packing up?" Tag suggested. "I'll take the gelding and scout around a bit."

"How's the stallion?" she asked.

"Ornery as ever," Tag said and blew out a breath.

"He just has to get used to you."

"He didn't seem to have any problems getting used to you."

"I had sugar cubes," she said.

"I think he likes you."

"That's kind of silly, don't you think? He's a wild animal."

"Wild animals have feelings too."

Lana shook her head. "Why don't you go on? I'll pack up the rest of the camp. You can tie the stallion to the back of the gelding." She paused. "He will go, won't he?"

"Yeah, he'll probably wait until we release him before he works hard to get free."

"When will we release him?"

"After you get your money," Tag said. "Then I'll take him back to the Bar M and release him in the breaking corral."

"Are you going to hurt him?"

He looked at her with concern in his deep brown eyes. "Do you think I would?"

Her heart skipped a beat. "No," she said and kept eye contact. "I don't believe you would."

"I'll break him slow," Tag said. "I promise. I want to keep his spirit, just control it."

"Tag."

"Yes?"

"What you did . . . I mean, how you talked him out of the pit. It was amazing. I know why they say you are the best horseman in the county."

He shrugged and she thought she saw a bit of a blush on his cheeks. "It's a talent I have."

"Well, it's a good one." She paused. "You deserve the reward. You know I couldn't have captured him myself."

"We stick to our agreement," Tag said and gathered his stuff. "You put the bridle on him, so you did your fair share. I couldn't have pulled him out of that pit without it."

"So we're partners," Lana said.

"Yeah," Tag agreed and paused to look at her. "We bring him in together."

"So I'll get the money and you'll keep the horse."

"That's what we agreed to, right?"

"Right," Lana answered, her heartbeat speeding up. He was so handsome standing in the entrance. She knew she could look at him the rest of her life and feel her heart kick.

He broke the spell by putting on his hat. "I'll be back in about thirty minutes. Will you be ready?"

"I'll be ready."

"Good," Tag said and looked out at the sky. "We need to get out of here before even more snow falls." He was gone before she could reply.

Lana held her blanket around her and studied the stone walls and dirt floor of their shelter. It was cold and primitive, but she would miss it. As much as she didn't want to admit it, she would miss Tag most of all.

"Just get your money and get out of Wyoming," she muttered. "Before you do something stupid and end up dying out here like your mother."

It was almost sundown two days later when Lana and Taggart reached the homestead. The trip had gone quickly when they had gotten out of the snow and into the lower altitudes.

They hadn't said much either. It was a bit of an unspoken thing. If they didn't talk about what happened up there, it would be easier to forget. Easier to move on.

Lana had to keep reminding herself that she wanted to move on. Wyoming had brought her nothing but despair. The money from the stallion's capture would bring her a chance to escape, and escape was what she had dreamed of for more than five years.

She glanced over at Tag. He rode the gelding with such expert ease it was as if he'd worked with the animal for years. Lana swallowed. It felt like she'd known Tag for years.

They should be happy. After all, they had both gotten what they set out for over two weeks ago. She would take the reward and move her father out of Wyoming and the constant reminder of his wife's grave. Tag would take the stallion to stud on the ranch he dreamed of owning.

They had both won. So why did she feel like her heart was breaking?

Chapter Ten

"Well, this is it," Lana told Tag as they reached the edge of her father's land. "The house is about a mile southeast."

Tag looked around. "Nice place."

"If you have cattle," Lana said. "We lost most of ours in the blizzards."

"Did your pa ever try to raise horses?"

"Pa never got over my ma's death," Lana said, her tone soft. "We haven't gotten much but a few potatoes out of the place since."

Tag lifted his hat and resettled it on his head. His breath steamed up in the dying light. "When you go to leave you'll probably want to sell the place."

"Hmmm," Lana said. She hadn't thought that far ahead. "I guess I could get something for it."

"How many acres?"

"One hundred and sixty," Lana replied. "Highland and middle pastures."

Tag glanced at her. "Before you sell, give me a holler," he said gruffly. "I'm looking for a spread to get started."

Lana had the sudden vision of Tag tending her ma's grave. His big, gentle hands pulling out the weeds. "Okay," she said with a lump in her throat. "I'll let you know first."

"Good," Tag replied.

"Town's about five miles due east," Lana said. "Just keep the border ridge over your left shoulder and you'll get there."

"I'll see you tomorrow then."

"Okay, we meet at noon in front of the sheriff's office," Lana said and watched him turn the stallion toward town. He got a few feet away and she became desperate to keep him with her. "Tag?"

He stopped and turned toward her. "Yeah?"

She couldn't keep him. She knew she couldn't. She had to leave Wyoming and he had to stay. It would be wrong for her to take him to San Francisco. Tag was pure cowboy, born and bred in the wild. It was as wrong for her to ask him to go with her as it would be to take the stallion. She blew out a breath. "You and the stallion will be there waiting for me, right?"

Tag eyed her a moment. Then he reached into his pocket and pulled out his whittling knife. "Here," he said and handed it to her. "It belonged to my grandpa. Now I know it's not worth two grand but it's all I've got that was his. You keep it so that you know I'll be waiting for you to collect the reward."

She took the pearl-handled knife. It was warm from his hand and smooth to the touch.

"Be careful with it. It's sharp."

She smiled. "I remember. Thanks."

"I'm the one who should say thanks. You saved my life, remember?"

"That was only one time," she said. "I believe you took care of me the rest of the time."

"So we're square, right?"

"Yeah," Lana agreed. "We're square."

"Good."

"Fine."

Tag kicked his horse into a trot and the stallion followed behind, the rope bridle barely controlling him. Lana's heart felt light and she kicked her mare into a run. She was going home with her goal won and her dreams blooming.

Lana dismounted and walked her mare to the corral attached to her father's barn. The homestead was quiet in the early evening. She figured her pa would be half sloshed by now and looking for his dinner.

She really wasn't up to facing that just yet, so she unsaddled her mare and brushed, fed, and watered her. Before too long she had done everything she could do.

It was time she faced her demons. The horses let out a complaint when she latched the gate to the corral. She smiled and patted her mare on the nose and told her it would be all right.

Then she took a deep breath and headed for the house. The porch angled down on one end. Pa had said he'd fix that one of these days. At least the screen door was hung proper. Lana knew that because she was the one who'd repaired it. In the last few years she had gotten good at making repairs—even those normally reserved for men.

She pushed open the door and entered the dim house. "Pa?" she called as she reached for a lantern and lit the kerosene wick. The lamp sputtered to life, illuminating the kitchen. It was surprisingly clean and neat. In fact, it was as if her father hadn't stepped foot in the room since she left.

A chill went down her spine. "Pa?" Still no answer. She moved to the parlor. It too was neat and cozy. Logs were stacked near the fireplace. Someone had placed a small bouquet of flowers in a glass jar on the end table.

Her pa's chair sat empty. His crocheted throw was folded neatly and tossed over the top. Lana frowned. What happened to her pa? She made her way to the bedroom. The door was open and when she peered in. The bed was made.

Now she knew something dreadful had happened to her father. There was no way he had made the bed. Lana had made it for him every day since her Ma had died. Jeff Tate hadn't had enough interest in life to think about making the bed.

"Pa? Are you here?"

The only place left to look was the small loft where she slept. Lana climbed the hand-carved ladder to the top of the cabin. Her room was neat, but dusty. It was clear that she had been the last person in there.

She sat on the edge of the loft. The house had grown dark and silent as a tomb. Maybe pa had gone into town. She took a deep breath and hoped so. It wasn't like him, though. He usually didn't go very far from the house and her mother's grave.

"Pa?" she called again from her position on the edge of the loft. There was no answer. She blew out a breath and swallowed her panic. He was probably at her mother's grave.

Lana went outside again. The wind was cold. A taste of snow was in the air. She rubbed her forearms and hurried through the dark to her mother's grave. It sat at the foot of the mountain under a large oak tree.

Lana sighed. Her pa was no where in sight and the grave looked like it had been awhile since anyone had tended it. She wondered if her father had left after she did. Sadness filled her heart. Her father needed taking care of and she had run out on him. It had been a risk for a better life, a risk she thought she should take.

Lana reached out and brushed the fall leaves off her mother's headstone. "I'm sorry, Ma," Lana whispered. "I really didn't think he had it in him to leave." The memory of her father's last words floated through her mind. "You leave me and I'm dead," he had said.

"He can't be dead," Lana vowed. "I have the money to move us to a better place. I won't let him be dead now."

She shivered as the swirling wind climbed down her back. She glanced up at the sky. It was a clear night and the stars stood out like a million diamonds on black velvet. Lana knew that Tag was under the same sky and everything would be all right. If she hadn't found her father by morning, she'd ask him to help her. If anyone could track her father down, it would be Tag.

Satisfied, Lana walked back toward the house. Her stomach grumbled and she realized that she hadn't really eaten all day.

When she reached the house she took off her coat and tied on an apron. Then after priming and pumping water into the sink, she washed her hands and began a simple stew of potatoes and carrots and a piece of ham that was hanging in the larder. She was up to her elbows in biscuit dough when the kitchen door burst open.

She jumped and grabbed a nearby knife.

"Lana, you're home."

Lana blinked. The man standing in the doorway was tall, clean . . . and grinning from ear to ear. "Pa?"

"I'm sorry I wasn't here to greet you, baby girl, but I didn't know when you'd be coming home. Heck, I didn't know where you'd gone, but Irene—I mean, Mrs. March—told me not to worry. You had your head on straight."

"Pa?" She couldn't believe it. Her father was clean and sober and smiling at her with clear eyes. Like she hadn't seen since her mother died.

He grinned and grabbed her around the waist and twirled her. "Daggum, I'm glad you're back. I've been searching high and low for you. You scared the living daylights out of me."

"Pa?"

"Yes, it's me, quit saying my name like some sort of parrot." He set her down. "Honey, I swear I've sent out search parties after you. Why just this afternoon I had the Palmer boys up near the—"

"Pa, I told you I'd be back."

"And you are, thank heaven. Sit down, sit down."

"I'm making biscuits."

He took her floured hand and pulled her to a chair. "Lana, I have something to tell you and it probably won't be easy for you to hear."

"Okay."

"Honey, I'm in love."

"What?" Love was the last thing she'd ever expected her father to say.

"I said I was in love. When you left, I thought you would never come back. I thought I had chased you away with my drinking, and if that's true, I'm sorry."

"Pa, I didn't leave because of your drinking. Well, not just because of your drinking."

"I know, Irene—I mean Mrs. March—told me she thought you had other reasons. Anyway, I decided I'd been trying to die for too long. Now it was time to think about living again. So I went out to the horse trough and doused my head in cold water and swore to the Lord that I would never take another drink in my life."

"Pa!"

"Yeah, I know, the good Lord about kilt me with

retribution, but I survived it. In part because of you. You sent an angel to watch over me. That angel is Irene March. The first moment I saw her I thought I'd died and gone to heaven, only I hadn't expected heaven to hurt so bad." He played with his shirt-sleeves. "When I explained to Irene that I had decided to get sober and go search for you, she stood by and helped me. She is a kind woman. I have no idea how you found her."

"I met her in the general store. She needed work and I needed someone to watch you while I was gone."

"Well, then it was the good Lord at work, sweetie. That woman has made a world of difference. When she first came by I could barely speak. She took care of me just like you said, and when I could stand again I figured I owed her, so I took to stopping by her place and doin' odd jobs around the house for her."

"Pa, we have a lot of odd jobs that need doing around here."

"I know, but I figured I had to pay her back first. Then I started looking for you, honey. I've been scouring the countryside. No one knew where you went."

"I didn't think I was gone that long."

"Over two weeks," her father chided. "I thought you were dead and I would never forgive myself if you had fallen to some harm because of me."

"I've been in the backcountry, Pa," Lana said. "I set out to capture a stallion and win a two-thousand-dollar reward."

"Why would you do that?"

"So that we would have money."

"You know money never meant that much to me or your mother. To think you could have gotten killed! All for money. Now, I know I didn't bring you up that way."

"You didn't," Lana said. "But I wanted the money."

"Why?"

"I thought . . . well, I thought I would take the money and move us to San Francisco."

"What the heck is in San Francisco?"

"Doctors who could help you," Lana replied, "and warm houses and better jobs and . . ."

"Yes?"

"There's an opera house in San Francisco, pa. I thought maybe I could sing there."

He smiled then and touched her cheek. "You are so much like your mama. She would be proud."

Lana touched his hand as a tear formed in her eye. "Are you proud of me, pa?"

"I'm proud, honey, so proud of you, and I'm so sorry I hurt you all those years with my drinking. I swore off the bottle for good, now. I promise."

Lana smiled. "Then I have good news."

"Tell me, pumpkin."

"I won the reward, pa," Lana said. "I captured the stallion."

"You mean that legend they keep talking about in town?"

"Yeah," Lana said. "I'm going into town tomorrow and collect the reward. Then we'll have enough money to move to San Francisco. You can get a good job and

I can sing in the opera house. Oh, Pa, it'll be wonderful."

Jeff Tate put his hand down. "Lana, I asked Irene to marry me, and she accepted."

Lana swallowed hard. "Oh."

"We planned on a quiet wedding once I found you. Nothing fancy, mind you, but something to celebrate."

"Are you going to live here?"

"No, I'm going to live at the Marchs'—well, soon to be the Tates'." He grinned. "It'll be okay, Lana, I went down to the land office and put this place in your name. I know you will take care of your ma's grave for me. Oh, and don't you worry, I talked it over with her and it's all right. I swear your ma was smiling down at me."

"Pa." Lana's heart took a dip. "Pa, I want to go."

"What?"

"I want go to San Francisco. I want to audition for the opera house. I want to live where there are carriages and gaslights and telephones and all the things I read about in ladies' magazines."

Her father looked at her.

"Pa? I said I want to go live in San Francisco."

"Well, honey, if you feel so certain . . ."

"I'm certain, Pa," Lana said. "I want you to go with me."

"Oh, baby." Her pa pushed the hair out of her eyes. "I guess you do have some of me in you. But I can't go. I have commitments here."

"You really love her?"

"Yes."

"She makes you happy?"

"Very."

"I suppose I can go by myself," Lana said. Her heart was heavy. When she left Wyoming she'd be leaving more than she ever imagined she would.

"If going to San Francisco is something you want that bad, then you should go," her father said. "But I want you to know that the ranch will still be in your name and you will always have a home to come back to should you change your mind."

Lana threw her arms around her father. "Thanks, Pa," she said. "Thank you for understanding."

"Now," Jeff said. "I see that you came straight home and started cooking. You must be tired from your adventure. Let me finish those biscuits for you while you rest. Even better, let me draw you a bath."

Lana looked at her father as if he'd grown another head. Heck, she felt like he was a stranger to her.

He laughed. "I do know how to make biscuits," he said and stood up with a wink. "Your ma taught me, too." He grabbed her hands and pulled her up. "We can celebrate with a nice dinner and a good bath. You go on upstairs and get out the tub. I'll start the water heating on the stove."

"But . . ."

"I can handle a few biscuits," Jeff said. "And stew is better the longer it cooks. Now go on upstairs. I'll bring the buckets up and fill the tub."

"But . . ."

"No more buts. You go on up and get out the towels. I'll have the first buckets of warm water by the time you're finished."

He pushed Lana toward the stairs. She moved like she was told, but stopped at the base of the stairs and watched her father humming as he readied the bath water. It was the strangest sight she had ever seen, but it brought back a vague memory. One of her father preparing her bath when she was little. A tear formed in her eye. She had left home and a miracle had happened. Her father had come back.

She sniffed and hurried up the stairs. Maybe after a good bath and a solid meal, she'd feel better. Maybe even ready to accept the topsy-turvy turn her world had taken.

The closer Tag got to town the more uncomfortable he became. Lana had gone home alone. How did he know that her father was even sober? Who would be there to care for her? If her father was dead drunk, any number of thieves or murderers could come and hurt her.

Pictures of Lana being hurt by evil men ran through his mind. He couldn't take it any more. Tag pulled the horses around. He'd just make sure she got home okay, he reasoned. Then he'd head to town.

The warm bath was bliss after a month in the back-country. What bathing she had done had been in cold streams. The warm water soothed her sore muscles and calmed her confused mind.

Irene March was a very nice woman. Lana had met

her in the feed store six weeks ago. They had been the only two women among the men and they had bonded instantly. There was something endearing about Irene's round face and apple-pink cheeks, something irresistible in her smiling eyes and no-nonsense speaking.

Lana should be happy for her father. But she wasn't, and she couldn't figure out why. Maybe it was because she was jealous. Maybe she wanted to be the one to skip out of the house and go running off to a new life.

It was hard for her to believe that a man of his age would do such a thing. She shook her head and hoped that Mrs. March had better luck with him than she did.

Then she thought about how happy he looked. How clean and energetic he was, and she knew her father would be all right without her.

That saddened her more than she wanted to admit and made California look farther away than she knew it was.

There was a pounding noise from outside. Lana sat up and clutched the edge of the tub. She heard her father put the last of the biscuits into the stove and head for the door. The noise sounded like hammering. Lana reached for a towel.

She could hear her father speaking to someone else. There was a heated exchange and then silence. Dread eased down her spine. Who would be out this late at night?

She dried off quickly and put on a clean but worn lawn dress. She climbed down from the loft, her feet bare and her dress buttoned only enough to keep her decent. Her heart pounded and panic rushed through her. There was no further sound from the porch.

Had something happened to her father? Lana grabbed a pistol out of the side drawer loaded it, and headed for the door.

"Who's there?" she called through the door. She kept the gun cocked and ready in front of her.

The pounding began again and she knew something was wrong. Lana pushed the door open and swung a lantern out. The light hit and circled back on a large pair of shoulders that moved with the hammering and the top of a very dark head that she knew well. Lana's heartbeat raced in time with the hammer.

"What are you doing?" she asked. Taggart Morgan looked up and wiped the sweat off his forehead. His eyes twinkled in the lantern light.

"I'm making this place habitable."

"It's habitable already." She stepped out onto the porch and eyed his work. He had fixed the sagging corner. "What do you care anyway?"

"I don't want to fall through the porch while I'm sleeping."

"What?!"

Jeff Tate stepped around the side of the house. "I told the boy he was welcome to sleep on the porch since he was kind enough to fix it."

"But . . ."

"No, buts, child," Jeff said in a tone she hadn't heard in years. "Now go on inside and put something on your feet before you catch your death of cold."

Lana gaped at her father, then glanced at Tag. Tag

grinned at her, looked her over from head to toe, and winked. She realized then that she was only half dressed. Embarrassed, she closed her mouth and went back into the house. It was clear the men were ganging up on her. It was something she just wasn't used to.

Chapter Eleven

Lana went straight to her small loft and righted her clothing. Pulling on thick socks, she muttered to herself about the unexpected appearance of Taggart Morgan and worse, the rush of excitement she felt when she realized who it was.

She pushed her feet into her pair of good half boots. They were usually reserved for Sunday dinners, but she refused to put on the same boots she'd worn for a month. It was time Tag saw her as she really was—a rancher's daughter.

Lana brushed her hair and wove a bright blue ribbon through it. Then she pinched her cheeks to add color, took a deep breath, and climbed down the ladder and into the kitchen.

The pounding had stopped and she glanced out the window. Tag had his back against one of the columns that held the roof to the porch. He was busy whittling

147

something with an outrageously large knife. The sight was so comforting that she sighed. The sound startled her. She could not go all soft on the man. He was her business partner and ornery enough to drive a woman mad. She had to remember that.

Lana pulled on a crisp white apron and wrapped it around her waist. Then she set the table and pulled the biscuits out of the oven. The smell of warm bread and thick stew made her stomach growl. It had been a long time since she'd had a proper meal.

She stepped out onto the porch and rang the dinner bell. Her pa would come in from his chores when he heard it. She glanced at Tag as he looked over his whittling.

"Did you eat dinner?" she asked. She tried to sound business-like, but the words came out tinged with concern.

"Nope," he answered as if she'd just asked him if pigs flew.

"Would you like to have some?" she inquired with tart sweetness. "It's just a simple stew, but it's ready."

Tag jumped up and pulled his hat off his head. He was heartstoppingly handsome, and uncivilized or not, he knew enough to take his hat off for dinner. "Is it okay with your pa?"

"My pa is a generous man," Lana answered and studied the horizon. "He'd let a pig in if it showed up hungry on our porch step."

"Maybe I should wait and ask him myself."

Lana whirled on him. "You'll do no such thing. Now come in for dinner or . . ."

"Or what?" he asked a twinkle in his eye.

"Or I'll never forgive you."

"May I wash up?"

"Certainly," she said and waved toward the door. "The sink's on the right." He moved next to her and she found herself relishing his clean scent.

"After you," he said and held the door. Lana knew it was all for show. Tag simply wanted her father to think he was a gentleman.

"Thank you," she said. If he could act like a gentleman, she would show him up by being more of a lady.

Tag seemed to take up a lot of room in the little kitchen. He was big and solid and she smiled, not believing he was really here.

"Dinner ready?" Jeff asked as he walked in and met Tag at the sink.

"I'm putting it on the table now," Lana said and set the bowl of biscuits down.

Jeff wiped his hands on the towel and waved toward a chair. "Sit, son, and enjoy some good cooking. My baby girl is one of the finest cooks in the county."

Tag sat and looked at her out of the corner of his eye. "Do tell," he said and stuffed his napkin into his shirtfront. "There's nothing better for a man than finding a gal who can outcook him."

Jeff chuckled. "It doesn't take much to out cook me."

"Well," Tag said. "We'll have to see how Lana stacks up next to me."

Lana gave him an evil look and set the pot of stew

abruptly on the table. Really, the man knew she could cook. How many times had they traded off the chore?

She sat down with a huff and patently ignored both men. Instead, she picked at a biscuit.

"So, are you one of the Bar M Morgans?" Jeff asked.

"Yep," Tag said and forked up some stew. "My brother Trey runs the Bar M. I'm more a horseman, myself."

Jeff glanced at her. "You don't say."

"Tag's known as one of the best horsemen in Wyoming," Lana said. When her father cocked his head and gave her a quizzical look, she shrugged. "That's what I heard in town."

"If you're looking for good stock, I have some of the best breeding mares around," Tag said. "They're all bred for endurance and strong footing in the mountains."

"So," Jeff said through a mouthful of succulent stew. "You're the one who helped Lana catch that stallion."

Lana glanced at Tag. He raised an eyebrow at her and deliberately put his elbows on the table. She glared at him and he ignored her. "Lana and I have a deal," he said, evading the question. "She gets the two-thousand-dollar reward and I get the stallion."

"I see," Jeff said and glanced at his daughter. "Nice of you to do that."

Tag forked up another mouthful of stew and caught Lana staring at him. She did not look happy. He shrugged and swallowed. "I guess I'm just that kind of guy."

"Stop it. We both worked together to catch that horse," Lana cut in. "Tell him, Taggart. Tell him I'm the one that put the bridle on him."

Tag let silence drift around them a moment, then he took a long drink of water. "That's right, Mr. Tate," Tag said and set his cup down. "Lana helped catch that stallion." He paused. "Yep, Lana was the first to put a bridle on the wild stallion that eluded the best horsemen in the state, and she did it all by herself."

"I see," Jeff said.

Lana's eyes flashed. "I did and you know it, Taggart Morgan."

Tag gave her an innocent look. "That's what I said."

"That is not what you implied."

"Now, you know I don't imply anything," Tag said. "I'm a straightforward kind of guy."

"Of course you are," Jeff said. Then he pushed away from the table and patted his stomach. "I'm full, baby girl. Thanks, it was wonderful. Now if you two will excuse me. I'm going to run over and check on Irene. I'll be back in less than an hour," he added, eyeing Tag.

"I'll be bunked down on the porch," Tag replied. "I'll leave a light on so you don't trip over me."

"Good." Jeff stood up, reached down, and gave Lana a kiss on her cheek. "I'll be back soon."

"Okay," Lana said and sent Tag a look. "Don't worry, Pa," she added as he walked toward the door.

"There's a loaded pistol in the drawer. I'll use it if I need to."

Her father put on his coat and hat. Tag swore he saw the older man grin. "Use it if you have to, baby girl," he said, opened the door, and paused. "I know I taught you how."

Then he walked out and closed the door behind him. The cabin rang with the sound of silence and Lana and Tag were alone.

Lana got up and took her dishes to the sink. She turned to gather her father's dishes and ran into Tag. He was a big strong wall that she wanted to lean into. Instead, she huffed. "What are you doing?"

"Helping," he said sort of low and near her ear. It made gooseflesh rise on her arm.

"Oh." She eased around him as he put his dishes in the sink next to hers. Then she escaped to the table and made a fuss about picking up her father's dishes. It seemed the kitchen had shrunk. She had to brush past Tag to get back to the sink.

He took a chair and turned it around and sat down, leaning his arms across the top.

Lana put the dishes down, grabbed the boiling teapot off the stove, and poured water over them. Then she added soap and pumped in enough cold water to cool it down.

When she couldn't take him watching her any longer she turned toward him. "What are you doing?"

"Watching you." His dark eyes glowed with some unknown emotion that skittered along her skin.

She brushed her hair out of her eyes with the back of her hand. "Why?"

"I like to," he said with a slight shrug.

A thrill raced down Lana's spine and she decided it was best to simply ignore him. She turned, refilled the kettle, and set it back on the stove so that she would have hot water to rinse the dishes. She put all of her energy into scrubbing, but she was aware of Tag's every breath.

"Your father's different than I imagined," Tag said finally.

Lana was happy to latch onto some bit of conversation that would settle the heat lightning in the air. "Pa's changed since I was gone. He actually said he's given up the bottle."

"What made him decide to do that?"

"I guess when I left to go after the stallion, he got worried and knew he'd have to be sober if he were going after me."

"So you did what you set out to do."

"What's that?"

"Change your life."

Lana put the last of the dishes in the rinse bucket and turned, leaning against the countertop. "I hadn't thought of it that way."

He studied her until she blushed and turned away. Lana busied herself with rinsing the dishes. A thought popped into her mind. She wiped her hands on a towel. "You said you were interested in buying the ranch. Are you still interested?"

"You going to sell it?"

"Yeah," she said. "Pa's going to get remarried."

"Congratulate him for me."

"I will," Lana said and blew out a breath. "He put the ranch in my name. So I can do whatever I want with it."

"You want to sell it?"

Lana thought about her mother's grave resting under the big tree. "To the right buyer I would."

"So you're still leaving Wyoming."

"Yes," she said and looked into his eyes. "Pa said I should follow my dream."

"I see."

"He said he was sure I would be successful."

Tag stood up and put the chair back in its proper place. "Honey, I don't doubt you'd be successful at anything you put your hand to doing."

"So are you interested?" Lana asked a bit too brightly.

Tag glanced around the room. "This the main house?"

Lana straighten her spine. She had to fight down the indignation she felt at his words. "Yes," she answered. "It has piped-in well water, a good-sized bedroom off the kitchen, and then there's the loft."

He looked up. "Is that where you sleep?"

Lana nearly choked. She cleared her throat. "Where I sleep is irrelevant." She moved to the door. "There are also several outbuildings including a smokehouse, the well house, the barn, and corral."

"Anything else come with the place?" he asked as he reached for the doorknob.

"I suppose you could keep the furniture. I doubt I'll need it in San Francisco."

"I guess that answers my question," Tag said and opened the door. Then he put his hat back on his head. "Good night, Lana," he said and closed the door with a soft click.

Lana stared at it a moment, wondering what he meant.

"You can leave that pistol in the drawer," Tag said through the door. "You'll go to bed safe tonight."

Lana stepped back quickly, embarrassed that he knew she was still standing so close. She emptied the sink and went up to her room.

Tag sat outside on the porch and listened to Lana prepare for bed. He whittled away at the bird that he had begun the night before. His thumb was still sore and probably would be for a few more days, but the wound was clean.

He glanced up into the night sky. It was cold and clear and full of stars. A thumbnail moon hung low against the mountains. It was a beautiful place. The rolling hills were wooded and the well water good.

There was a lot a man could do with a spread like this. But that house needed a woman inside, one with sweet blond hair and small capable hands.

Lana awoke to the silver-pink of morning slipping through the small window in her loft. She rolled over and sighed. Things had changed while she was gone.

Her father had discovered a new reason to live. The

ranch was hers to sell or keep, and she was free. The only person she had to look after now was herself.

It was kind of scary, but freeing as well. If she wanted to, she could move away and her father would be fine, even the land would be fine. Tag would take good care of it. She rolled over and pushed the thoughts of Taggart Morgan out of her mind. Now was the time for action. Thoughtful action ruled by the mind, not the heart.

It didn't matter that she found his fear of needles endearing. It didn't matter that she loved to see him handle a horse. That she liked having him in the kitchen watching her.

She shook her head to rid herself of the image. Now was her chance to leave, and she would be stupid not to take it.

Lana dressed in her Sunday best. A girl wanted to be at her prettiest when she was to be the talk of the town. She pulled out a pale blue gown with tiny white roses embroidered on it. The fine lawn felt good against her skin. She slipped on the dress. It had a nice bustle, not too large, draped with white lace that matched the roses. It had long puffed sleeves and a square-cut bodice. It might be a bit out of style, but she had always felt like a princess in it.

She knew that Tag was still around. He had promised to see she got her money and she knew he would.

He had never seen her at her finest. She wondered what he would do. Would he look surprised? Would he like the way the tiny green leaves next to the roses matched the color of her eyes?

She brushed and fixed her hair into an intricate knot. Then she pinched her cheeks, grabbed her best coat and her leather riding gloves and went downstairs.

She was too excited to eat breakfast and fairly flew out of the house, nearly knocking Tag off the porch. He caught her around the waist.

"Whoa, what's the hurry?"

"It's time to go into town."

He set her on the ground and held her at an arm's distance. "You look . . . beautiful," he said quietly.

A blush warmed her cheeks and her heart. "Thanks."

He let her go. "I got the old beast ready. Your mare's saddled too, so whenever you want to go."

"Let's go now. I can't wait to see the look on the men's faces when I bring him in. I mean, *we* bring him in." She turned and made her way to the horses. "You know, he really should have a name."

"A name?"

"Yes, old beast isn't nearly as dignified as say . . . Chester."

"Chester?" She swore he choked on the name.

"What's wrong with Chester?"

"Doesn't sound very . . . regal to me," he said diplomatically. "Got any other ideas?"

She reached her horse and he bent and helped her mount. The feel of his hands on her waist was wonderful. They were big and warm and protective and still a little dangerous. A thrill ran through her. She tried to ignore it.

"Other ideas?"

He mounted his mare and they headed down the road. "How about Champion?"

"Champ? Sounds like a dog."

"What about Beau?"

"Now that sounds like a dog. What about Prince William?"

"Too stuffy."

"Albert?"

"That's ridiculous."

"Ridiculous? What's ridiculous about Albert?" she asked. The stallion whinnied as if to ask the same.

Tag leaned on his pommel and eyed the horse. "What about Blackie?"

"Blackie. Sounds kind of average. He is, after all, an extraordinary horse."

"Yes, he is extraordinary."

"I know," she said brightly. "Let's call him Maximillian."

"Maximillian." Tag sat up. "Not bad. I can call him Max."

"Good, Maximillian it is."

"Right, Max."

It was going to be a long way into town, but the bright sunshine and the warm autumn air buoyed Lana's spirits. She looked beautiful. Tag had said so. The look in his eyes rewarded her efforts to look her best.

Feeling like a queen, she started humming. By the time they reached town she was singing, and Tag joined her. He had a nice voice. His tenor played in perfect harmony with her soprano.

People came out of their homes and businesses to see what the heck was going on. Lana didn't care because they all knew she could sing. Now they would know that she could catch a horse.

They stopped in front of the saloon. The reward had been set by the saloons in Hunter, Amesville, and Boonstown. All three towns wanted bragging rights for the capture of the stallion.

Tag got down and tied his horse to the waiting post. Then he helped Lana down, but the stallion protested being in town. It was all Tag could do to keep him in hand.

The commotion brought the townspeople out. The entire saloon emptied onto the sidewalk and the street. Lana stopped with a flush of excitement.

"Mr. Mayor," she proclaimed when Doc Bodie stepped out of the crowd. "We're here to claim the reward for the capture of the wild stallion and to claim victory for the town of Hunter."

Instead of cheering, her proclamation was met by silence. "What do you mean you've come to claim the reward?" the mayor said.

"Taggart Morgan and I have brought in the stallion," she said and waved her hand toward Tag. The stallion snorted and rolled its eyes at the crowd. "And we would like our two-thousand-dollar reward."

"Who's to say he's even the stallion?" someone shouted from the crowd.

Tag shook his head. "He's the old beast. A few years back Jack Ryan took a potshot at him, remember?" The crowd murmured its remembrance. In fact the whole county had been mad as hornets at Jack. He'd had to move to Cheyenne after that.

"This here stallion has a graze scar on his right hip." Tag pointed out the scar.

"How'd a little thing like her help you capture him?" Chance said as he elbowed his way to the front of the crowd. "You can barely keep hold of the animal now."

"Now that's a story," Tag said. "Let's take the stallion to the stables and I'll tell you all about it."

The crowd followed behind Tag and Lana as they wrestled the wild horse into a stall in the stables. The stallion didn't like to be cooped up. He snorted and pounded the stall, but it was too sturdy.

"The crowd has him all stirred up," Tag said and took off his hat and wiped his forehead. "Let's get out of here and go get a drink. I promise I'll tell you all the story."

"It's better be a good one," Chance said and eyed Lana. "I've got money riding on the outcome."

"You're just going to have to give up that money, Chance," Lana said and lifted her chin.

"Let Tag tell the story," came a cry from the back.

Tag grinned and strode across the wide main street to the saloon. "It's some story, all right. Seems some guy named Gooding dug a series of pits around the old man's watering hole."

The crowd grumbled at that idea. Who would do such a terrible thing?

"I got there first, of course," Tag went on. The

crowd muttered agreement and Lana had to bite her tongue to keep from reminding them that she had an active part in the capture. "Well, it snowed and I didn't see the traps. My mare stepped right into a deep hole."

People gasped. "I know," Tag said. "Her left leg snapped when she fell and she came down on top of me, pinning me to the ground."

"How'd you get out?" someone hollered.

"Now that's where the story gets good," Tag said. "Why don't we all go inside and finish this story over a drink?"

"Tag Morgan's buying," someone else hollered. "He's the one with the two-thousand-dollar reward."

"But—" Lana began.

Tag covered her mouth with his hand and waved the crowd in. "Keep quiet," he whispered. "I'll take care of everything."

Aghast, Lana gave him a dirty look and tried to bite his hand. But Tag was very quick for a big man. He was gone before she could do anything. He glanced back at her with a grin as he patted the mayor on the shoulder and ushered him into the saloon.

The crowd disappeared inside and she was left alone in the street. She decided then and there that she was going in after her money. Unfortunately, the crowd was so big it blocked her way inside. She tried to push through to no avail. All she heard was oohs and ahhs and whoops of celebration.

Lana kicked the man nearest the door, but he didn't even budge. Instead he was grinning ear-to-ear as someone handed him a free drink.

Lana knew then that she wasn't going to get in. She reached into her small purse and pulled out Tag's pearl-handled whittling knife. Then she glanced at the crowd.

She had no choice, really. She had to trust him.

Chapter Twelve

Tag found Lana in the stables. She sat on a bench beside the stall where he had placed Max. His whittling knife lay in her lap.

Tag's heart skipped a beat. She looked deflated. She had her elbows resting on her knees and her chin cupped in her hand as she studied the stall across from her.

"Hey," Tag said.

"Hey," she answered and glanced at him. "Are you done entertaining the whole town?"

"Yup," Tag said and leaned against the stall. He studied her for a full minute. Her pale hair had once been neatly put up, but now had slipped out of the bun and down her slender back. He remembered what it was like to hold her and lie next to her under a star-filled sky. His hands ached to touch her skin. He knew it was smooth and soft.

163

"I suppose they gave you the reward."

"Yup," Tag said.

She sat back against the stall and sighed. "They don't believe I helped, do they?"

He was silent. He wanted to tell her that they did believe. That they all cheered her and drank to her health, but it would be a lie.

She stood up. "I thought so."

"The money's still yours," Tag said and pushed the purse toward her.

"I can't take it. They gave it to you."

"We both know I couldn't have caught him without you," Tag said. "They may have handed me the purse, but that doesn't make the money mine."

"I suppose it's better that they think you caught him," Lana said and took the purse. "That way your reputation will still be intact."

"I don't care about my reputation," Tag said and he realized that he didn't. Somewhere along the way Lana had become more important than his pride.

"You should," she chided. "A reputation is about all a person has in small-town Wyoming."

Tag noted how she sad her tone was at the mention of this small town. "So now that you have the money I suppose you're going off to San Francisco."

"I suppose I am."

For some unexplained reason the thought of losing Lana hurt. Confused, he mentally shook off the pain.

Lana glanced at the stall. "Well, that's that I guess."

"Yeah," Tag said. "That's that."

She turned to go, then stopped. "Just one more thing."

"Yes?" His heartbeat sped up. Would she kiss him one last time?

"I want to tell Maximillian good-bye."

"Oh, sure." Tag reached over and opened the small door at the top of the stall gate.

The stallion stuck his head out. He rolled his eyes and nodded. Then he inhaled deeply and snorted.

Lana smiled at the animal and reached up to pat his head. Tag held his breath. For all he knew the old beast would take a chunk out of her hand.

To his surprise, the stallion tolerated Lana's touch. "Good-bye, Max," Lana said softly. "Thank you for the adventure."

The stallion nudged her shoulder. She pulled a sugar cube out of her coat pocket and held it out on a flat palm. The animal took the sweet, then pushed her with his nose. Lana backed into Tag. He slipped his hand around her waist and held her against him.

She smelled like fresh air and sunlight. Her silky hair caressed the back of his hand, and he knew that he never wanted to let her go.

He leaned down and planted a kiss on the side of her neck, on the sweet spot just behind her ear. She leaned back against him and he held her tight. The sound of horses stomping filled his ears. The sharp smell of hay wafted through the crisp air.

Lana, sweet Lana, leaned against him, allowing him

to hold her against his heart. He wanted to stay in this position forever.

It seemed an eternity before she stepped away. Her warmth left with her, leaving his heart cold and sore. He cleared his throat and studied the door to the stall. "Are you going to leave right away?"

"Yeah," she said. "With pa getting remarried there isn't anything keeping me here."

"When are you going?"

"Soon, I guess. Why? Are you still interested in buying the ranch?"

"Yeah, sure."

"All right. There's just one thing."

"What's that?"

"I want you to promise me that you'll look after my mother's grave."

Tag's heart hurt more. His own mother's grave was very important to him. "That's a pretty big responsibility."

She looked at him with liquid eyes that touched his soul. "I know you're up to the task."

He told himself not to touch her. If he touched her now, he would ask her to stay. If she stayed, she would always wonder what would have happened if she had followed her dream. He didn't want to be responsible for that.

Tag took a step back.

"I'd like to ride the property line before I buy it."

"Be my guest," Lana said, and turned and gave the stallion one last pat on his handsome nose. "I would expect nothing less from you."

"So I'll see you around then," Tag said and walked away. If he could have, he would have run.

Leaving turned out to be the hardest thing Lana had ever done. Her bags were packed. The house cleaned and polished. She held the train ticket in her hand as she looked out over the rugged horizon.

When it came right down to it, Wyoming was a raw but beautiful place. Tag had been right. The air was clean and sharp and stirred your blood.

The first snows had come and the trees were stark underneath the gray sky. The wind blew cold against her cheeks. Lana tied on her new winter bonnet, fastened her wool traveling coat, and stepped off the back porch.

Her mother's grave was a mere mound under a blanket of white, sparkling snow. Lana brushed off the headstone. "Well, Ma, I'm going off to live my life now."

The shrill cry of a hawk split the air. Lana looked up. The hawk circled the forests in search of food. The sight was at once brave and lonely. Lana's heart swelled. That's how she felt, brave and lonely. She patted the headstone. "Tag will take good care of you. He's the best man I have ever met," she confided. "I think you'll like him. I know I do."

"Lana!"

She straightened and saw her pa coming across the yard toward her. He had married Irene March two days after she returned. Lana knew then that he would never go away with her. If she were to do this, she was to do it alone.

"I have to go, Ma," Lana whispered and fought the tears welling in her eyes. "I have to see if there is more to life than wide open spaces and wolves howling in the night."

"Lana, Taggart's here to take you to the train station."

"I'm coming, pa!" She hollered back. Then she touched the headstone one last time and walked away.

The Tate place was a real bargain. Taggart had tasted the sweet water and heard the whispering of the aspens and cedars. It was close enough to his brother's ranch that he would never be lonely, yet gave him enough range to breed horses. The house needed some repair, but it was sound and well insulated against the icy wind. There was just one thing missing.

Lana.

Lana's beautiful voice haunted him. Her smile and expressive eyes filled his dreams. He'd spent every day of the last week at the ranch. His excuse was he wanted to get a jump on the weather, but he'd spent most of the time watching her.

Lana doing laundry. Lana humming as she dusted. Lana cooking. Her sleepy eyes when she got up early in the morning and took care of the animals.

He watched her crossing the yard. She looked like a snow queen in her new hat and coat and muff. He hadn't ever seen her as happy as she was this week. She had shared with him her plans and dreams for her new life. Her joy had been his sorrow, but Tag held his tongue.

He didn't want her if she didn't want to stay.

"Ready?" he asked and put her trunk into the back of the wagon.

"Ready as I'll ever be," she said.

"Good," her father said and gave her a big hug. "Do you have everything? Your ticket? The directions to that place you're going to stay?"

"Yes, Pa, I have everything." Lana smiled. "I have the train ticket and the directions to Mrs. O'Malley's boarding house. She assured me it was modest but in a solid neighborhood."

Her father hugged her again. "I'm going to miss you. You be sure and write, and remember, if you ever want to come back . . ."

"I know, I know, there's a place for me."

"That's right. Now you'd best get going or you'll miss your train." He helped her up onto the wagon seat and held his hand out to Tag. "Thanks for taking her to the train. I'd go, but it looks like Irene's milk cow is going to drop her calf."

"It's no trouble," Tag said and shook his hand. "That's what neighbors are for."

Tag climbed up onto the wagon seat and snapped the reins. Lana waved until they rounded a bend and her father was no longer in sight. Tag was aware of her every move.

They rode in silence for a long time. The wagon wheels crunched through the snow and the sharp air kissed their cheeks. Lana was all pink and cream. Her new hat framed her face. She took a deep breath and blew it out.

"Nervous?" he asked.

"A bit," she admitted. "I realize that I'm going to miss this place after all. It was the longest we'd ever stayed in one place."

"Because of your mother?"

"Yes," Lana said. "Now with pa taking on a new family, I doubt he'll ever leave Wyoming."

"So you'll come back to visit."

"I suppose I will."

"Then it's not really good-bye. Is it?"

"No, I guess it isn't." That seemed to cheer them both up.

The ride to the train station went fast. Too fast, Lana realized. She enjoyed talking to Taggart. She enjoyed just being in his company. When they didn't speak the silence was comfortable.

Lana had taken the opportunity to memorize the way his wide shoulders moved and his arm muscles worked as he drove the wagon. She had inhaled his scent, and it brought back memories of when he held her in the stables, when he tucked her in under the rainy canopy in the backcountry.

She was torn. As much as she wished her father were going with her, she wanted Tag to go even more. Doubt filled her. Maybe she shouldn't go. Maybe she was making a big mistake.

Tag loaded her trunk on the train and walked her to

the small set of steps that led up into the car. Lana chewed her bottom lip.

"This is it," Tag said. "You have a good trip."

Lana turned toward him and looked up into his eyes. "Tag?"

"Yes?"

"Can you give me one good reason to stay?" Lana held her breath. She didn't know what answer she wanted from him, but she had to have an answer.

He studied her, his gaze growing distant and mysterious. "No Lana," he said. "I can't."

She stood there. The sounds of people saying their good-byes, the rattle of the train, the clang and clack of trunks and bags being loaded filled her ears. The sound of her heart pounded in her head.

Tag nodded, stepped back, and tugged the brim of his hat. "Go on now," he said, his voice oddly gruff. "Go explore the world."

Lana swallowed her fear, her doubt, and the sadness in her heart. "Right." She turned and let the conductor help her up. She did not look back. She was afraid if she did he would be gone.

Tag's heart hurt in ways he could never express, but he knew he had done the right thing. He had let her go. His mother had once told him that he couldn't hold a butterfly in his hands no matter how bad he might want to. When you held something that delicate too close you could kill it without even knowing.

It would have been selfish to keep her in Wyoming just because it was what he wanted. He knew it had to be what she wanted, and right now she didn't know what she wanted. She was frightened enough taking that step toward her dreams. He didn't want her to stay with him now only to leave later, or worse, to regret she had stayed.

Tag watched the train until it went around a distant bend. Then he turned and mounted.

He had done the right thing. So why did it hurt so bad?

Months passed and the stallion worked Tag harder than any horse he had ever broke, but it had been worth it. He knew he had a horse of legendary proportions. The breeding potential alone was enough to set him up for a lifetime and make his ranch prosperous.

But he'd never moved into his ranch house. He couldn't live there knowing Lana wasn't there. Still, he kept his promise and went daily to care for her mother's grave.

His brothers often asked about his trip, the horse, and where he went when he left. He never answered. He'd simply walk out. They soon left him alone.

Today, as he rode through the pasture, Tag realized that spring was coming. The sun was out and the snow completely melted. The ground was soft and smelled of things beginning to bloom.

He wondered how he had gotten through the darkest days of winter. He couldn't remember much except the part where he pitted his will against the stallion. The first few weeks without Lana had been hell, and the stallion's fight had given him something to concentrate on. Then one day the animal quit fighting and Tag was left with a feeling of emptiness.

It was an emptiness he couldn't explain.

He glanced at the mountains and realized the snow was retreating. Maybe it was time for him to get on with his life, time to settle into his new ranch.

In the distance he saw a strange carriage parked near the ranch house. Curiosity got the best of him. He'd told no one that he owned the place, so he never had visitors.

It wouldn't hurt if he checked out what was going on. He approached from the south. The carriage shone in the spring light. He could see that it was small and smart and new. It had a mare attached, a mare that looked familiar.

Max paused, snorted, then took off at the scent. Together they jumped two fences and hurled themselves to a stop in the yard. Tag jumped down and approached the carriage.

It was a beauty, trimmed in mahogany and leather. The horse pulling it was quiet and sweet and Tag patted her. He knew her, this horse. She belonged to Lana.

He was afraid to hope. He told himself it was just Lana's pa come back to visit his first wife's grave. He did that on occasion. It was simply that he had never brought Lana's mare with him.

A figure stood at the gravesite.

His heart leapt into his throat. It was Lana. She was dressed in a new wool coat. Her hair was done up like a society woman's and she wore a new-fangled hat, but she was still Lana and she had come back. He tied Max to the hitching post and strode across the yard.

A twinge of fear stopped him. Could he stand to see her one more time, knowing she would probably be leaving again?

Could he stand not to see her?

Her hair tangled in the wind, like hands beckoning him forward. She wore a peacock-blue dress under her coat and coal-black half boots. Her hair took on a halo effect in the sunlight.

Tag finished the distance between them.

"Hello," he said.

Lana turned. A beautiful smile lit her face and Tag had all he could do to keep still. Her skin glowed in the sunlight. Her eyes were clear green gems, and her lips, polished rose. She took his breath away.

He had to remind himself that it had been months since he'd last seen her. She could have a beau in the city. She may not even think about him anymore.

"Hello, Tag," she said. Her hands held a bouquet of flowers in bright spring colors. "How are you?"

"Making do," Tag replied.

He drank in the sight of her. She looked even more beautiful than before. Yet there was something different. She seemed more confident, more self-assured. "It looks like that big city has done you good."

"Thank you," she said, a sweet blush rushing up her cheeks. "I'm sorry to intrude. I knocked on the door, but you weren't there."

He glanced at the house. It looked as empty as his heart had felt. "I haven't moved in yet."

"Oh." She fiddled with the flowers. "Why not?"

He shrugged and reached up and tucked a stray hair behind her ear. He couldn't help himself. He couldn't be this close to her and not touch her. "It seemed too empty." He wanted to tell her he missed her. He wanted to tell her . . . heck, that he loved her.

That thought shocked the bejesus out of him. He stepped back. He needed a moment to think this through. Of course he loved her. That was why he'd let her go. He couldn't stand the thought of her not loving him in return.

"I missed you," he said, "and the house reminded me of you."

"I missed you too," she said softly.

"Tag—"

"Lana—" They spoke at the same time.

She smiled at him. "You go first."

"No," he said gruffly. "I might not be a gentleman, but I know that ladies should go first."

"I learned a lot about myself and this big wide world we live in."

"So you found your dream?"

"Yes," she said. "I came back to tell you that I found my place in the world."

Tag's heart sank. He didn't move. He didn't want to reveal the pain her words caused. "I see," he said. "I suppose you've found yourself a man to love."

"Yes," she said with sincere eyes. "I've discovered that I'm in love. Deeply in love."

Taggart wasn't sure if he would ever breathe again. He swallowed. "He's a very lucky man."

"I'm the lucky one," she went on. "I'm in love with a sweet, gentle man. A man who brings me comfort and passion. A man who vexes me with his stubbornness. A man who claims to be uncivilized but knows enough to let a lady go first."

Confused, Taggart frowned at her.

"Taggart Morgan," Lana said and took a step toward him, "I'm in love with you."

It took a moment for her words to sink in. He blinked.

"Tag?"

"Yeah?"

"What were you going to tell me?"

Tag took off his hat and scratched his head. She loved him. He didn't quite know what to do. "Lana, I think you may have just gotten yourself into something you may regret."

She stiffened. "I see," she said, her mouth pinched. "I'm sorry." She moved as if to leave.

"No, wait!" he said and took ahold of her arm and drew her toward him. "I just realized that I love you too, Lana Tate. I love you too, and it scares the pants off me."

"Oh, Tag." She fell into his arms. "It scares me too. Let's be scared together."

The kiss they shared healed the sore spot in Taggart's heart. She was warm and sweet in his arms. He wanted nothing more than to pick her up and take her away.

So he did.

"Taggart Morgan!" she exclaimed and grabbed him around the neck. "What do you think you're doing?"

"I'm taking my woman into our house," he replied. "Where I fully intend to love her forever."

Lana flung the flowers into the air and rained kisses on his face. The flowers landed near her mother's headstone, and somehow she knew her mother was smiling down on her.

Epilogue

They were married a few days later in the small church in Hunter where Lana sang on Sundays. The family gathered for a party after.

Lana passed around another plate of cookies. The house teemed with people. People who she could now call family.

Tag had invited all his brothers. Trey Morgan came in beaming. He introduced her to his wife, Brianna, and their boys. The boys had doffed their hats, said hello, and then dove into the platters of cakes and cookies that Lana and her new stepmother had made. They pushed and tugged each other until they tumbled out the door. Brianna smiled.

"Please forgive them," Bri said. "They don't get to attend too many parties."

"The cookies are wonderful," one boy said shyly. Another boy rushed by and grabbed the shy one.

"Don't mind him," the second boy said. "Chris is just angling for extra cookies." Chris smiled and winked at her. Lana noticed that his pockets were bulging.

Matthew and his wife, Sam, had come. Matt looked so much like Tag it startled Lana. Then he took off his hat and she saw that he had blue eyes, not dark ones. Samantha gave her a hug and whispered in her ear, "These Morgan men can be a handful sometimes. Send for me if you need some help." She leaned back and smiled. "We love them but sometimes it helps to have backup."

Lana smiled at that. She liked Sam right away. "I'll keep that in mind."

"Matt, don't let your wife corrupt my Lana," Tag said and put his arm around Lana's waist. She looked up at him and smiled.

Samantha tsked. "Take my advice: Don't even think about spoiling him. Give in once and it's all over."

"Hey!" Matt complained. Sam smiled at him. There was a squeal of delight and Samantha turned and chased after her toddler. "Amy's almost two and the boys have spoiled her silly," Matt explained. "I feel sorry for the man she marries."

Lana glanced at the beautiful curly haired baby. "I don't," she said quietly.

"Come on, Lana," Tag said. "You have to meet my brother, Shay."

Tag took her out on the porch. There was an impromptu game of cards going on. A tall, thin blond man was teaching the game of poker to three of the four March children. "Shay, quit corrupting minors and come meet my wife."

The handsome man winked at the kids and stood. "Hello," he said and held out his hand. "It is always a pleasure to meet such a beautiful woman."

Lana blinked. He took her hand and kissed it, then looked at her with soulful eyes. He had the face of an archangel, and Lana suspected he could be just as fierce.

"Does she have any sisters?" Shay asked Tag and glanced inside the house.

"Nope," Tag said with pride in his voice. "I got the only one and I happen to be very happy about it." Lana blushed at the conversation.

Shay winked at her. "Too bad," he said and put his hand over his heart. "If my brother ever gives you any trouble, you just come see me," he said. "I'll be happy to help you. Now, do I get to kiss the bride?"

Tag pushed his brother. "Keep your hands to yourself."

Shay raised his eyebrows at her and bowed deeply over the hand he had yet to release. "Don't forget," he said and kissed her fingers. "I'm always at your service." Then he let go of her hand. "Did I hear there were cookies inside?"

Lana watched him hold the door open for one of the other ladies and then step into the crowded house. "Are you sure he's your brother?"

Tag shook his head. "I've got to apologize for him. He's the black sheep of the family."

"The black sheep?"

"Yep. Ma got to him first. Gave him too much education and taught him manners. Then when Ma died Matt and I promised her Shay would go to college and make something of himself."

"Did he?"

"Of course, we figured he was already ruined. We might as well finish off the job."

Lana smiled. "I like him."

Tag frowned and put his arms around her waist. "Not too much I hope."

"Nope," she said and reached up to touch his face. "I've found I really have a taste for uncivilized men. Tame ones bore me."

He hugged her tight and kissed her full on the mouth. The kiss was filled with joy and promise.

"Hey, cut that out," Jeff Tate called. "There's children around."

Tag winked at her. "Later."

She blushed. They had a lifetime of laters, and she trusted they would be just as wonderful as today.

Lana turned and looked out over the yard. Children were playing tag. Her father and Irene walked hand in hand. Early flowers had popped up between the patches of snow. The great Teton Mountains loomed over them all, wise and mysterious.

Tag kissed her temple. "A penny for your thoughts."

"I was just thinking about how much my life has changed since I met you."

"Any regrets?" he asked cautiously. "Are you sure there's nothing waiting for you in San Francisco?"

"No," she said and held him tight. "No regrets. San

Francisco is a very large city. Too large. The people there don't really care about each other."

"What about the opera?"

"Right, the opera. I got hired as an understudy."

"You did? That's great. I knew you were good."

"Being an understudy was a real eye-opener," she shook her head. "I watched the stars flit from party to party trolling for the man with the most money, and I learned something very valuable."

"What's that?"

"I learned that my ma was right all along. Fame and money are fleeting. Love, on the other hand, is the most precious thing of all."

"Hmmm," Tag said against her temple. "I told you she seemed like one smart lady. Now come on." Tag took her hand and pulled her off the porch.

"Where are we going?"

"Someplace a little more private."

"What about the family?"

"They're perfectly capable of taking care of themselves." He pulled her into the stables where he had Max saddled and ready. He mounted and then pulled her up behind him. "If we're lucky no one will see us," he said and wiggled his eyebrows.

Lana laughed and put her arms around his waist. They got as far as the other side of the barn before one of the boys noticed and the race was on. No one was as fast as Maximillian and soon they were alone.

Tag took them to the top of a ridge and dismounted. He pulled her down into his arms and turned her toward the view. They could see for miles and miles.

"The whole world is at your feet, Lana Tate Morgan," Tag said. "What are you going to do now?"

She smiled a secret smile. "I'm going to love you, Taggart Morgan. I'm going to love you."

They kissed and Tag let go of Max's reins. The stallion shook his head and wandered off to search out the fresh growth of new grass.